D1412311

The Lost Boy of Triletus

(Book 1 of the Tales of Triletus)

By
Wally Larson, Jr.

This is a work of fiction. Names, characters, places, and incidents are products of the author's imagination or are used fictitiously and are not to be construed as real. Any resemblance to actual events, locales, organizations, or persons, living or dead, is entirely coincidental.

Copyright © 2020 by Wallace ("Wally") Lee Larson, Jr. All rights reserved.

Cover art by
Sebastien Theopold Peiffer

ISBN: 9798616538109

DEDICATION

To my parents,
Margaret and Wallace ("Wally") Larson (Sr.),
authentic beacons of hope, joy and love

Dedication disclaimer:
This dedication is solely an homage and does not imply their endorsement of
any aspect of this book.

CONTENTS

1 HOW TO RAISE A SON
WHO CAN RULE

Once upon a time, High King Axel and Queen Gwyneth reigned over all worlds from The Place Without a Name. A son was born to them, named Creedon, and they proclaimed him the Crown Prince of the realm of Triletus, a prized jewel among their kingdoms.

When Creedon was born, Their Royal Highness' Fairy Corps rejoiced to know that Triletus would someday be ruled by the Prince. However, the Whisperer secretly began to plot the boy's destruction.

The Whisperer was a fairy who was once chief of the Corps (he was known as Maddox at that time). But Maddox attempted to use his power to usurp the throne for himself. While certain fairies followed him in that rebellion, the majority of the Corps stayed loyal to the High King and Queen, so they reported his rebellion to them while also helping to resist it. The Royals ejected Maddox from his position but continued to allow him to roam their realms and even appear in their presence at court. They hoped that their mercy would, someday, be rewarded with his renewed loyalty.

Maddox became known as the Whisperer because he was too clever to challenge the Royals' authority directly. Instead, he would whisper intrigue to others in an ongoing attempt to disrupt the Royals' reign.

The Fairy Corps and others who served the court could not understand why Their Majesties did not send the Whisperer into exile; why they continued to put up with his mischief. But they deferred to Their Majesties' superior, though mysterious, judgment in this matter.

One day the Whisperer (who had wings and, like other fairies, was about the size of a hummingbird) arrived when the court was discussing the future of the Crown Prince's reign over Triletus. The Whisperer raised a discordant note. He said, "Please forgive me if I am speaking out of turn, Your Majesties. But I can't help but wonder, how a boy who grew up sheltered in your palace could possibly rule over those with whom he has no common experience."

The royal advisors and members of the Corps began to hiss at the Whisperer's suggestion, but the King waved them to silence saying, "Peace, please, we shall hear him out."

"Thank you, *good* king," said the Whisperer in a tone that expressed the opposite. "I mean only to ensure that your subjects in Triletus are ruled by someone who has walked in their shoes. Someone who has experienced their every-day challenges and so can maintain and even improve the realm."

Queen Gwyneth nodded and said, "How would you propose that we address this concern?"

The Whisperer had slyly anticipated this question. The Whisperer said, "Send the boy to live in Triletus without the trappings of royalty. Rather, give him a true education by having him live as a commoner in his formative years. Then, he will truly be qualified to rule over his subjects."

Although the members of court were unhappy to hear the High King and Queen giving consideration to this proposal, they could not contest its merit.

The High King said, "I have no illusion, Maddox, that your true motive is to serve this court or the subjects of Triletus. Nevertheless, we will send the boy to live in Triletus. We will identify a humble couple in a small town of the realm. That couple will raise him until he is eighteen years old. Upon achieving that age, he will then travel about the realm until he is ready to rule."

"That sounds like a very wise course of action, High King," said the Whisperer with a crooked grin. "But what will you do about the boy's knowledge of his own royal status and also about his gift of magic? Surely such knowledge and gift would make him unable to *truly* live as other Triletians live."

"He is who he is," said the Queen, "and just as Triletians struggle to steward their own knowledge and gifts, Creedon will learn to struggle through that as well. We will instruct him not to divulge his royal status while he is still a boy. When he reaches the age of eighteen, then he will use his own judgment as to when and what to disclose. He will learn, as you already know well, Whisperer, that disclosing his royalty will bring the opposite of honor or welcome."

The High King and Queen dismissed the Whisperer and called Creedon into their presence. When he arrived, they told him what they planned for him to do. To the boy's credit, he did not complain or attempt to argue. But all those gathered at court could see how much the idea of leaving the palace pained him.

"Young Creedon," said the High King, "we give you a heavy burden to bear. Until you reach the age of eighteen and begin to journey throughout Triletus, you will not be permitted to publicly disclose your royal status as our son. Some will, however, inevitably guess the truth when they discern your noble bearing and your gifts. You should use discretion as to how and when you employ your gifts, especially magic. To begin, we will send you to a good couple who will adopt you as their own. Once you reach the age of eighteen, you will then have latitude who to tell that we are your parents and that you are their Crown Prince. At such time, you will also be forced to leave that home and village. You will experience a new level of animosity as you travel around Triletus, but I will send you two helpers from another world so that you are not alone.

"When the time is ripe, then we will proclaim your rule to the realm. For too long, Triletus has viewed this court as a figment of legend. Only rarely has a member of the Fairy Corps been able to make contact with a citizen. But one day you will be the face of our royalty for all Triletians."

Creedon bowed and said, "Of course, I will obey. But will I be able to see you at all while I'm gone?"

His parents looked at each other and sighed.

"Perhaps, rarely," said the Queen, "but we will have to see how things go. We will always be watching from here and thus, always with you in that sense."

Brightening, the High King said, "But tonight we will celebrate the beginning of a new chapter in our family's life with revels. We shall have the best food and drinks, with music and our best storyteller to entertain. Then, tomorrow morning, we will bid you farewell."

If you have ever been to a good-bye party for someone, then you know how bittersweet the celebration was. Creedon sat between his parents throughout the evening, and they whispered to him guidance and encouragement as it occurred to them. The storyteller, who through magic could tell stories of the future, was enlisted to tell the court a story of the future in Triletus. The story described a time when the realm's two leading city-states would be unified through a wedding. You can read it in the second tale of Triletus.

2 A LOST BOY
ON THE DOORSTEP

The next morning, Creedon awoke after a wonderful dream that he could not remember in detail. He could only recollect vague images: a deep blue river that led to a waterfall and a lush green field where sheep nibbled at vivid blades of grass.

There was a knock on his door, and an attendant poked his head in to say, "Shall we proceed, your Majesty?"

"I'll be right there," Creedon said. He packed a small bag, as his parents had instructed, and then he returned to the throne room where the High King and Queen sat alone. After eating breakfast together, the Royal Parents stood and embraced him for a long moment that Creedon wished would not end. But he knew it was his responsibility to break the embrace, and so he finally did.

"There now, I'm ready," Creedon said.

The High King and Queen took their seats and then said, "Peace and honor be with you, son."

As they faded from view, Creedon found himself standing in stormy darkness. As he blinked his eyes, he could make out the door of a modest home through the raindrops. There was a small sign over the door that said, "The Evergreen." He knocked: once, twice and then a third time.

The door opened, and a kindly woman's face looked down upon him. "Good evening, young man," she said, "how can I help you?"

He looked down at his feet, unsure of what he was to do or say, watching the raindrops splash upon the toes of his boots.

When the woman realized the boy was soaking wet, she hurriedly said, "Please forgive me, come in out of the rain, we can talk inside!"

Gratefully, he followed her inside and, after asking the woman's permission, carefully put his bag down just inside the door. He also removed his hooded cloak, placing it upon a nearby peg to dry.

Inside, he could see a man sitting by the fire and smoking a pipe while reading a book entitled "Healthy Triletus." The man looked over his reading glasses and said with feigned annoyance, "What you have brought in out of the rain this time Helen?" In truth, he welcomed the diversion; it was a quiet village with excitement in short supply.

"This is . . . . I'm sorry, I don't know your name, young man," Helen said as she ushered Creedon to a chair by the fire.

"Thank you, ma'am. Sir, my name is Creedon."

"Hello, Creedon," said the man. "My name is Galen and you've already met my wife, Helen. Where do you come from?"

"I, uh, come from a place far away," said Creedon.

"What do your parents think about that?" asked Galen, intrigued. "You look to be nine or ten years old, yes?"

"Yes, I'm ten years old, sir. My parents sent me here."

"*Sent* you?" Helen said as she seated herself. "Why?"

"They sent me because they felt it was necessary for my future. I am to stay here until I turn eighteen years old."

"What do you mean by *here*?" Galen asked. "*Here* as in this village or *here* as in this house?"

"Both, sir, I guess, come to think of it," said Creedon. "They specifically sent me to the *two of you.*"

Galen and Helen both sat quietly for a moment, taking this all in. Then Galen spoke up, "Please don't take this the wrong way, son, but what did your parents expect us to *do* with you?"

"They didn't tell me that, sir," said Creedon, "but they assured me that you would know what to do. Do you have children?"

"No," said Galen quickly, knowing this to be a sensitive issue for his wife. "We had hoped to have children, but after years of trying we concluded that it was not meant to be. I wonder if your parents knew that when they decided to send you to us?"

Helen seemed far more sanguine about this situation than Galen. "So, Creedon" she said, "you have nowhere to stay tonight, correct?"

"That's correct," Creedon said, "I am very sorry to impose upon you in this way. It sounds like no one warned you I was coming . . ."

Galen took a puff on his pipe and expertly blew out small puffs of smoke. "In one sense," he said, "we had no warning. But in another sense, you could say that we have had multiple warnings over time." He looked knowingly at Helen before continuing: "Well, we certainly cannot send you out into the rain this evening. If you would like, you can sleep here tonight and then tomorrow we can talk about what to do next."

"Thank you, sir," said Creedon, "I am much obliged to you both."

"Nonsense," said Helen, "it is our pleasure to have a guest, in the midst of the storm no less."

She walked him to a spare room where she quickly made up the bed. "Are you hungry?" she said. "It sounds like you have journeyed a long way."

"I'm not hungry, ma'am, but thank you for asking. I had a large meal recently and will sleep well." Which was true. After the abrupt transition from morning breakfast in the palace to late evening here, he was feeling the emotional toll of already missing his home, his friends and his parents. He was soul weary and fell fast asleep. He dreamed of his home, of music, and of laughter with his parents. Of fun with members of the Fairy Corps.

As Creedon slept, Helen and Galen huddled to speak quietly by the fire. "Well, Helen," Galen said with a bemused look on his face, "what do you have in mind for our guest?"

"Honestly," said Helen looking into the fire, "I don't know. I think I'm acting on instinct here. A helpless young boy shows up on our doorstep, was sent by his parents from who-knows-where, and it's raining buckets outside. What else could we do?"

Galen nodded, more serious now. "Yes, you have a gracious heart my dear. As odd as this situation seems, somehow it feels like it was meant to be. Do you know what I mean?"

"Yes," said Helen earnestly, "I do. But what shall we do in the morning?"

"Perhaps," said Galen, "we could ask the boy if he has any plans . . . as a way to get to know him. We can take our lead from his answer."

"Fine," said Helen, "but you heard the boy, I mean, Creedon. He said his parents specifically sent him to *us* and that we would know what to do then."

"Yes," said Galen, "but that begs the question of *why* he was sent to us; for what purpose?"

"Suppose," said Helen cautiously, "that he says he was sent to *stay* with us; that we are to look after him?"

"If we get to that point," said Galen thinking out loud, "then we would have to bring him to the Almas Council. We can't have a child moving in here without any process or procedure; that would be highly irregular."

"Fair enough," Helen said, "and what would we ask the Council to do, specifically?"

"Hmmm." Galen pursed his lips as he pondered this, then said, "We could ask them for official approval of our temporarily acting as Creedon's guardians. Then we'd see how that goes before we ask for more."

Helen nodded, "Yes, that makes sense to me. I'm relieved to have a plan."

Galen gazed into the fire and said, "Why would loving parents send their son to live with a couple of poor medical doctors like us?"

Helen shook her head in silent response. But she was secretly glad to have a child around the house, if only for a short while. Surely his parents would come asking for him back at some point?

After they retired for the evening, Galen slept like a log, but Helen tossed and turned as she pondered the mystery of it all.

When they arose the next morning, Creedon

was already sitting in front of the newly lit fire. He had quietly crept outside to collect firewood and was looking into the fire intently, as if searching for answers.

"Good morning, Creedon," said Galen. Helen was in the kitchen making scrambled eggs with crackling bacon.

"Good morning, sir," Creedon said.

"How did you sleep?" said Galen as he blinked at the morning light pouring through the window.

"Very well, thank you for your hospitality," Creedon said.

"Time for breakfast!" Helen called from the kitchen. Galen and Creedon moved to the small table in the kitchen and joined Helen sitting there. Two small steaming iron skillets, one with eggs and one with bacon, sat waiting in the middle of the table.

"Please dig in," Helen said. His hosts let Creedon help himself to the food before they partook, and he ate voraciously. Galen and Helen looked at each other and realized that they had not planned which of them would raise the question with Creedon.

"So, Creedon," said Galen gamely jumping in, "what are your plans?"

"Uh, I really don't know," said Creedon. "My parents sent me here, but other than the fact that I'm going to start traveling when I turn eighteen, I don't know exactly what I'm supposed to do here in the meantime."

"Ok," said Galen slowly, "and you mentioned last night that you were specifically sent to *us*. Do you know if your parents intended for you to *live* with us?"

"Yes," said Creedon, "I think that's what they wanted."

"Funny that they didn't ask us first," said Galen wryly but Helen hushed him with a quick gesture. Without Creedon seeing, Galen made a motion that said, "Ok, your turn honey."

"Creedon," Helen chirped nervously, "if you would like to live with us for a while, we would welcome that. But we would need to submit this arrangement to the town's Council for approval, to ensure that they agree. How does that sound to you?"

"That sounds good," said Creedon happily between mouthfuls and oblivious to the adults' anxiety. "See, my parents were right, you *do* know what to do."

"We can head to see the Council directly after breakfast," said Galen, "but Creedon, you should know that the Council may have more questions about your parents and where you come from. We didn't want to interrogate you last night, but the Council will need to be comfortable that, for example, you are not running away from parents who are desperately worried about you somewhere."

"Yes, I understand that," said Creedon. "I will do my best to explain what I can."

When they were finished eating, Creedon helped Galen wash and dry the dishes and then they all dressed for the day.

As they walked out the front door, Creedon said, "By the way, what town is this?"

Helen said, "You are in the humble town – some would call it the village – of Almas."

"Is your house called The Evergreen? I saw that sign over your door last night," Creedon said.

"Yes," said Galen. "Folks here like to name their houses and sometimes they choose a type of tree for their home's name, as we have."

As they walked, Creedon looked around, trying to visually absorb as much as he could at once. He noticed that they were near the water, and saw wooden boats and fishing nets along the way.

Watching him, Helen said, "You are probably noticing that this is a fishing village. Most of the people here make their living by fishing or doing something connected to that."

"Is that true for you as well?" asked Creedon.

"Helen and I are the exception," said Galen. "We are both medical doctors. Do you know what that means?" Creedon nodded that he did.

"This is a relatively poor village, so people cannot afford to pay us much for our services," said Galen. "The big cities, like Sepadocia and Murta, already have many doctors, while these small towns often have none. Helen inherited The Evergreen from her parents when they passed away, and we took that to be a sign that this was the place where we should be."

As he said this they arrived at the town "gate" which was, in fact, just a sign by the roadside that said, "Welcome to Almas." Creedon's hosts explained that the seven adults sitting on chairs in a semicircle were the town's Council. Galen made a hand motion to request being added to the Council's docket, and someone in the Council with a pen and parchment gave a thumbs up as if to say, "You are on the queue."

The trio was able to sit and listen as the Council discussed matters of health and property, and then the Council secretary said, "Doctors Galen and Helen would like to be heard."

The couple ushered Creedon forward and, after taking a deep breath, Galen began to speak:

"Learned members of the Council: my wife Helen and I would like to introduce you to our new friend and guest: his name is Creedon. He knocked on our door last night in the middle of the storm, and we took him in as our overnight guest without asking too many questions. He has told us that his parents live far away and sent him off, without rancor and for a future purpose, to this town and specifically to us at The Evergreen. He said that his parents assured him we would know what to do when he arrived. His only additional guidance is that he is to live with us, at least until he reaches the age of eighteen. We obviously would not be comfortable acting as his hosts or caretakers for such a long period, or even another night for that matter, without submitting this to your authority," Galen said humbly.

"Thanks to you both for bringing this to us so promptly," said Marina, the chief of the Council. She was especially fond of this couple because of how they served the village as doctors when they could have chosen a much larger town as home. "I'm sure I speak for my colleagues when I say that this young man could not have chosen a better home in which to seek shelter. Do you and Helen have any specific proposal in mind?"

Galen deferred to Helen, who said, "We propose to take the next thirty days to act simply as Creedon's hosts. We would take this opportunity to get to know him better and learn more about him. Our goal would be to determine whether in fact he will *want* to live with us longer, and whether we feel that we can host him well. If so, we would come back to you with a longer-term proposal. In the meantime, while we don't know what kind of schooling he has had, we imagine that the Council would want him to be enrolled in school here so that his education is not neglected."

"Indeed," said Marina, "well said. Do any of my fellow members have a problem with this proposal?"

One member asked, "Could Creedon say any more about where his parents live? While I would like to be able to take his word for his parents' wishes, is there a way that we could confirm their existence and wishes in this matter? It all seems rather unusual."

Galen and Helen looked at Creedon and so Creedon rose to respond. "Yes, it is unusual for me as well," he said. "I apologize to the Council and to my hosts that I am unable to tell you who my parents are or where they live. My parents request anonymity."

The members of the Council looked at each other with shrugs, as if to say, "What else can we do?"

"Well, then," said Marina, interpreting the Council's silence as permission, "we shall proceed as Helen proposes. In thirty days we shall meet with the three of you again to hear how it's going."

Galen and Helen thanked the Council for their time.

"Come, Creedon," said Helen, "it's time we enrolled you at The Schoolhouse."

3 THE SCHOOLHOUSE

The only school for children in Almas was called, simply, The Schoolhouse. It had once been the largest residence in the village, but when its owners (former proprietors of the largest fishing operation in town) decided to move to one of Triletus' larger cities, the couple gifted the house to the town. The Council had wisely decided to convert the house into the home of the village's first school.

The house had five large rooms which had been easily converted into classrooms, with chalkboards and desks. When Creedon enrolled, the school comprised about sixty children aged from five to eighteen. They were divided into five age groups called "forms": five to seven-year olds (this group was called the "first form"), eight to ten-year olds (the "second form"), eleven to thirteen-year olds (the "third form"), fourteen to fifteen-year olds (the "fourth form") and then sixteen to eighteen-year olds (the "fifth form"). Each form used one of the rooms and had its own teacher.

When Galen, Helen and Creedon entered the foyer (entrance hall) of The Schoolhouse, all five classes were in session. An administrator greeted them from his desk in the foyer. He explained that it was rare for someone to enroll in the middle of the school year, but after Helen explained the situation, the administrator (a young man named Andreas) took it in stride. He said, "We usually administer a brief diagnostic test to determine a student's appropriate classroom. I know that Creedon is ten years old, but it can be useful to have a sense of where he is scholastically. Does that suit you?"

Helen and Galen nodded and asked Creedon if he would be ok taking the test on his own while they returned home to see patients. "Sure," said Creedon, "thanks so much to both of you, I will see you this afternoon."

Creedon sat in a small room alone while he took the diagnostic test. After perusing the first few questions carefully, he began scanning through the rest more quickly and came to a realization: he knew all of the answers. But, if he answered all of the questions correctly, he might be placed with the oldest age group and that would seem very odd indeed. What did the High King and Queen want him to do in light of his mandate not to disclose who he was?

"To intentionally answer questions wrongly

when I know the correct answer would seem dishonest," he reasoned to himself, "but if I leave the more difficult questions blank then at least that seems *more* honest." The questions were divided into sections which, though not labeled as such, clearly were segregated by age group. Creedon could tell which section would place him into the eleven to thirteen-year old group (the third form) and he decided that this would be the best group for him.

So that is how he proceeded with the exam. He waited sometime after completing the questions before handing it to Andreas (who was still at his desk out in the foyer), not wanting to seem too quick about it. To fill the spare time, Creedon had just stared out the window for a while. Andreas glanced through Creedon's responses, noting the questions that had been left blank.

"Creedon," said Andreas looking up from Creedon's exam, "what kind of educational background do you have?"

"I had a private tutor until yesterday," said Creedon truthfully.

"But you don't know where you come from?" Andreas said skeptically.

"I'm sorry, since it was my home from birth, I never was told that it had a name. I guess it's only when you *leave* a place that you really find you need a name for it, sir."

"I see your point," said Andreas begrudgingly. "I'm sensing that you could have answered the rest of these questions correctly if you wanted to, but I won't press you on that. Rest assured, we would not force a ten-year old to sit with the fifth form (the oldest age group) even if you were smart enough to do so. So, are you ready to meet your teacher?"

"Yes, sir," said Creedon nervously. The classes were all beginning their break, and as the students noisily ran outside to enjoy it, the teachers congregated around Andreas' desk with steaming coffee cups in their hands.

"Teachers:" said Andreas, "please say hello to Creedon, who is staying with Galen and Helen during his time in Almas. He'll be joining the third form." The teachers had plenty of questions in mind about Creedon's backstory, but they were polite enough to wait until later, when Creedon was not standing there, to pepper Andreas with them.

The third form teacher, Miss Mariada, shook Creedon's hand and said, "Hello young Creedon, welcome to The Schoolhouse. I'm Miss Mariada and I'll be your teacher."

Andreas handed her Creedon's diagnostic test, and after a quick glance at it, Mariada escorted Creedon up an elegant stairwell to the third form classroom on the second floor. As they passed other classrooms she called out, "That's the first form room," "there's the second form room," and so on. When they reached the third form classroom, she opened a beautiful carved mahogany door to reveal a well-appointed room with twelve student desks in two long rows of six.

She pointed Creedon to a small student's desk in the back right. "That will be yours for the time being; we'll see how that works. You will be sitting next to Charley, who is thirteen years old. Even though he's a few years older than you, I think that the two of you could get along well."

Just as Creedon settled into his seat, Andreas rang the bell in the foyer and the students all came clamoring back into The Schoolhouse. The third form students were rushing to their places in the classroom until they noticed Creedon and slowed to gawk at him.

"Who's that?" they whispered to each other.

Miss Mariada heard them and said, "Class, once you take your seats, I will introduce you to our newest student."

The six boys and five girls were thus motivated to swiftly take their seats. Miss Mariada wrote Creedon's name on the chalkboard and explained that he was new in town and would be living with Galen and Helen for a time. The students all knew of Galen and Helen, the only medical doctors in town.

"Please make Creedon feel at home," she exhorted them. "Imagine how you would feel if you came to live in a strange town far away from your own home, and were getting used to all sorts of new things and people at once."

Charley leaned over to Creedon and whispered,

"Do you like candy?"

Creedon nodded eagerly and Charley handed him a piece. "Thanks!" said Creedon happily.

Miss Mariada began a math lesson in which the children took turns going to the chalkboard to work out problems. Soon, with his mind focused on the lesson, Creedon found himself feeling less like the new, strange kid and more like he belonged.

At lunchtime, he learned that the school provided a family-style lunch at long tables in the dining room. The afternoon sessions flew by for Creedon until the closing bell rang to signal the teachers to finish up.

Miss Mariada asked Creedon if he could stay a moment after the other children left for the day.

"Bye, Creedon," said Charley on his way out the door, "I'll be outside playing for a bit so I may see you when you're done here."

The teacher asked Creedon the same questions that Andreas had asked: about where Creedon came from and so on. Creedon told her what he had told Andreas, explaining that Galen and Helen had brought him to the Council that morning and that the Council had approved his staying with his hosts for thirty days, after which the Council would evaluate the arrangement.

Miss Mariada pondered all of this and then said, "Creedon, if you had to guess why your parents sent you to Almas, what would you guess?"

Creedon considered what he should say, and

then ventured, "Well, I would say that there are certain things they felt I could not learn as long as I stayed at home. That in order for me to reach my full potential, I needed to come here."

"To this backwater fishing village?" she said with a hint of a smile.

"Yes, ma'am, to live with real people," he said.

"Oh, we're *real* all right," she said wryly. "Creedon, I sense a deep maturity and intelligence in you. Unfortunately, those qualities in someone so young can, at times, be threatening to others. I don't say this because I want you to be immature or to try to unlearn what you know. I just say this to caution you. Have you heard the phrase 'the nail that sticks out gets hammered down'? No? Well, do you at least understand what the phrase means?"

"I think I do," said Creedon cautiously.

"It means," Mariada explained, "that in Triletus generally, but perhaps especially in smaller towns like Almas, we have a curious dilemma: we all want to be unique individuals who stand out, but at the same time we feel a tremendous pressure to fit in. No one person decides how *much* uniqueness is a good thing; it's a group thing and thus difficult to assess as it fluctuates."

"For example," she said, "this Schoolhouse used to be owned by a married couple who ran the largest fishing operation in Almas. But, over time, the people of this village became jealous of their success. No matter how generous the couple was to the town, it only seemed to make things worse. Someone threw stones and broke their windows. Someone else broke into the house and stole artwork and other valuables. It's why the couple ultimately left Almas to live in a big city: they decided that they were always going to be viewed as nails that stick out here."

"Something tells me," she continued, "that someday you will feel pressure to leave Almas for the same reason. But, for as long as possible, I suggest that you 'keep your head down' – if you know what I mean. When you need to confide in someone, there's Galen and Helen, and there's also me. I sat you next to Charley because he has a good heart and can be a friend to you; I don't think he will be threatened by your gifts. But beyond that, *you* will need to figure out who you can trust."

She put a hand on his shoulder and said, "I'm sorry, Creedon, to lay such a heavy burden on you after your first day in class. But I feel that I should warn you now, before it's too late. Something tells me that your parents might have given you the same warning."

"Yes, ma'am," he said, "although I am only beginning to understand why."

She turned and began erasing the chalkboard but called over her shoulder, "Fear not, Creedon. On the bright side, certain people in Almas may pleasantly surprise you. But at the end of the day, you can only do what you can do. So long, young man; I'll see you tomorrow morning."

"Thanks, Miss Mariada, see you tomorrow," said Creedon.

Creedon walked out the classroom door and down the stairs, past Andreas in the foyer (who waved as the boy walked past) and out the front door. In the lawn outside, Creedon spotted boys and girls playing a game of kickball.

"Hey Creedon," said Charley, "come play with us."

"Sure!" said Creedon. He had not played kickball before, but he soon got the hang of it. He joined Charley's team and, for the first time since he'd arrived in Almas, he felt like a normal kid.

When the game was over, the boys left in one gaggle and the girls in another. As the boys walked down Almas' main street, the boys said good-bye, one by one, as they reached the turn-off for their roads to go home. Charley pointed to his road and asked if Creedon wanted to come over to his house for a bit.

Creedon said, "Sure, can I just let Mr. Galen and Miss Helen know? I could run to do that and be right back."

Charley said that was fine, so Creedon sprinted for The Evergreen. When he arrived, he noticed that there were people sitting outside on the porch, apparently patients waiting to be seen by Galen or Helen.

He took the liberty of skipping past these waiting citizens into the house and knocked on a closed door inside.

"Yes?" came the voice of Helen through the door. Creedon opened the door and poked his head in to see Helen sitting at a table with another woman, her patient.

"I'm sorry to interrupt," he said, "would it be ok if I play at Charley's for a while?"

"Of course," said Helen, "thank you for checking. Dinner at seven?" He gave a quick thumbs-up and quietly closed the door, sprinting back to Charley's. Almas was starting to feel like home.

4 A GLIMPSE OF MAGIC

Creedon ran at full speed to reach Charley's house, determined not to miss any fun. The house was in a heavily wooded area of town. As he approached the home's front yard, he saw that Charley was there with his two brothers, Nate and Paul (Creedon would learn that Nate was nine years old and Paul was eleven). The boys were sitting cross-legged in a lazy triangle in the grass as they debated what to do for fun. Charley waived Creedon over to join them.

"Hey Creedon, these are my brothers Nate and Paul." They nodded at each other. "We're trying to decide what to do," said Charley. "Do you know any good games?"

Creedon thought for a moment as his eyes wandered over the surroundings. He saw the sign over the entrance to Charley's house, identifying it as The Red Maple. The house was surrounded by trees and Creedon could see that behind the house there was a delightful creek with a trickle of water running through it; just enough to get your feet wet if your foot missed a stone in the creek bed and fell into the water. He quickly thought up a game to incorporate the creek.

"How about we play 'Creek Crossing,'" he suggested.

"What's that?" said Nate, sounding interested.

"It's pretty simple," said Creedon, who was making it up as he went along. "We divide into two teams, and one of us from each team starts on opposite sides of the creek and sees who can cross to the other side the fastest without getting wet. Each round, whoever crosses first wins a point for their team. Then whichever team gets five points first, wins."

The boys all nodded. Charley and Creedon formed one team, while Nate and Paul were the other team. Creedon was at something of a disadvantage, not being familiar with the creek, but even so he and Charley came close to winning. Huffing and puffing from the effort, the four boys shook hands all around. Then they sat down to rest on the rim of the creek farther from the house, with their backs to the woods.

The boys were all curious about where Creedon came from, so he gave them the same explanation he had given to the adults at school.

"Are you able to tell us *anything* about your home, even if you don't know the name of it?" said

Paul.

"Well, let me think," said Creedon. "It isn't a fishing village like Almas, but it has people and leaders and education and things like that. My parents are leaders there but they felt like I needed to come and live here for a while. So they must think Almas is a special place."

"Last year, Dr. Helen helped our dad recover from a terrible illness," said Charley, "so we feel like we owe her a lot."

"Do you know what kind of doctors she and Mr. Galen are?" said Creedon.

"Dad said we should call them *Dr.* Helen and *Dr.* Galen," said Paul. "I think Dr. Helen deals with stuff inside the body while Dr. Galen deals with things like broken legs and arms and things. I don't know the medical words, but Nate went to see Dr. Helen last year when he hurt his ankle in the creek."

Nate nodded to affirm this and proudly pulled down his sock to show a small scar on his ankle as proof.

They grew quiet for a moment, gazing up at the scruffy white clouds, buoyant in the Triletian blue sky. Then they heard a rustling behind them in the woods. They turned their heads to see the source of the rustling and then jumped to their feet once they did.

A giant brown bear was slowly lumbering towards them.

"Stay still, guys," said Paul quietly, "don't do

anything to provoke it."

They did stand still, but the bear continued to draw closer, aiming for Charley. Creedon remembered that Charley had candy in his pocket and surmised that the bear had caught the scent.

The bear was now just a few strides away from the boys. All four of them knew that their lives were at risk. Charley and his brothers remembered that their father was inside the house, but they didn't want to provoke the bear by yelling for him.

Creedon took one step backwards so that the other boys could not see him. They were so focused on the bear and frozen in fear that they didn't notice what Creedon was doing. Creedon silently held up his right hand to the bear as if to say, "Stop." The bear stopped in its tracks and continued to look at them. The other boys silently rejoiced but remained still, unsure what to do now.

"Charley," said Creedon softly, "why don't you throw the bear your candy. Perhaps that's all that he wants." Charley was so frightened that Creedon had to gently shake Charley's shoulder and say it again.

"Oh yeah, of course," said Charley. His hand shook as he pulled the candy out of his right front pocket. He tossed the candy with an underhanded motion so that it landed at the bear's front paws.

The bear made a kind of friendly growling noise as it picked up the candy and tossed the candy into its mouth. It stood up on its hind legs and, with its right paw, gave them a salute. Then it turned and lumbered back into the woods.

It took the boys a few seconds to believe that all was clear so that they could move again. However, once they were confident that the bear was not returning, they noisily clambered over the creek bed and into the back door of The Red Maple. Their father, a jovial man with a ginger beard, was sitting inside by the fire reading a book when the four boys raced in and slammed the door behind them.

"Dad, Dad!" called Charley and his brothers.

"Hello, boys," the man said as he rose from his chair, "who is your friend?"

Charley quickly introduced Creedon, and then the boys let Nate tell their father, whose name was Jasper, all about the bear.

"So, the bear stopped, just like that?" said Jasper, incredulous. "Bears don't often accost humans, but I've never heard of one stopping for no reason like that. I thought we had scared all of the bears off a while back, but I'm going to report this to the Council in the morning. We are *all* going to have to be more careful in Almas."

Jasper focused on Creedon: "Young Creedon, I am grateful that your first visit to our humble home did not end with tragedy. You are most welcome here any time."

"Thank you, sir," said Creedon. Spying a photo of Jasper with a woman, Creedon said to Charley, "Is that your mother?"

"Yes," said Charley. "She passed away last year

from a mysterious disease. Both Dr. Galen and Dr. Helen cared for her until the end."

"Oh, I'm sorry," said Creedon, "I didn't realize . . . "

"No need to apologize," said Jasper. "It's good for you to know, since you're our new friend. We grieved as a family when Sally passed away, and we still treasure the happy times we had with her. Death happens to us all, eventually."

"Dad," said Nate, "can Creedon have dinner with us?"

"Creedon, you're welcome to join us for dinner here any time," said Jasper. "But I imagine that Galen and Helen would like to get to know you, since you've only just arrived in town. There will be plenty of opportunities for you to eat here in the future."

"Thank you, sir," said Creedon, "this is probably a good time for me to go. I'll see you guys later."

Creedon sprinted to The Evergreen and entered the kitchen just as Helen and Galen were setting the table for dinner. "You're just in time," said Galen with a smile, "hopefully you like chicken?"

"Yes, Dr. Galen, chicken sounds great," said Creedon.

As they sat down to eat, Helen and Galen felt grateful to have a third person sitting with them for a change.

"Now Helen," said Galen after a swallow of food, "what are we going to have Creedon call us?

'Dr. Galen' and 'Dr. Helen' seem rather formal. We're not his parents, but we're also not his doctors . . . at least not yet."

"Quite," said Helen with a furrowed brow, "Creedon, your parents must somehow know of us and trust us, because they specifically sent you to us. So perhaps you would like to call us Aunt and Uncle, as if we are your parents' honorary siblings?"

"Yes," said Creedon, "that would be nice. I think that my parents would want us to live like we're a family."

"Then that's settled," said Galen. "How was your day?"

Creedon described his first day at The Schoolhouse. "They put me in the third form and Miss Mariada is my teacher. She's very nice and made me feel welcome. I sat next to Charley and after school we played kickball and then I went to Charley's house. We saw a bear!"

"A bear," said Helen nervously, "near their house?"

"Yes, Dr. Helen . . . I mean *Aunt* Helen. The bear was just on the other side of the creek in their backyard." Creedon decided not to describe the whole incident, lest it raise questions he wasn't ready to answer.

Helen and Galen gave each other a worried look. "Two years ago, a mother and child in Almas were attacked by a bear," said Galen. "Your aunt and I treated them as best as we could after the attack, but they passed away a few days later. Jasper – Charley's dad – may have mentioned that, as a result, the town opened season on hunting bears for a while. This is the first time we've had a bear sighting since then."

"Mr. Jasper said he's going to tell the Council in the morning," said Creedon, trying to be helpful.

"Good," said Helen firmly. The three of them chewed silently for a moment. Then Creedon spoke up, "So, you are both medical doctors?"

"That's right," said Galen. "In the past I have specialized in orthopedic medicine and Helen in internal medicine, if those terms mean anything to you. But since we moved to this village, we have both had to become generalists because there aren't any other doctors nearby."

"So, you haven't always lived here?" Creedon asked.

"No," said Helen. "We used to live in the wonderful city-state of Sepadocia. But villages like Almas began to send word to the large cities, basically *pleading* for doctors to come because they had none. As Galen mentioned earlier, my parents lived in Almas and left me this house when they passed away, so we felt a pull here."

"There was also the legend," said Galen.

"Yes, there was that," said Helen. "Creedon, as I think you know by now, this is the world – that is the realm – of Triletus. For a while now, as long as anyone can remember, Triletus hasn't had a ruler. These days, we have self-governed city-states, towns and villages, but that's it.

"Many Triletians believe, as we do, that there are a High King and Queen who silently govern Triletus. But we never hear from them directly and we don't know much about them or even whether they are in this world. Occasionally you hear a rumor that they have said something or done something, but otherwise it's generally just silence from them. Anyway, there is a legend that one day they will have a son – the Crown Prince - who will grow up in Almas and one day rule over Triletus."

"That legend was a reason that you came here?" said Creedon.

"Now that you mention it, I can't say we ever actually *discussed* it," said Helen looking at Galen. "But I think, unconsciously, that it was a reason for me."

"Yes, and for me as well," said Galen. "I think just the possibility that we might have the privilege of being in the Prince's home village was enticing."

"We like seafood, too," said Helen playfully, "and there's seafood aplenty here in Almas."

Creedon pondered all of this, and then said, "After class today, Miss Mariada gave me a piece of advice. She said that I should be careful about being the nail that sticks out."

Galen and Helen both nodded, interested. "Did she elaborate?" said Helen.

"She seemed to think that I have a special gift," said Creedon, "and that while using that gift should be a good thing, that it could also make people afraid or jealous. So that I should be, uh, 'discreet' is the word she might have used."

"A special gift, eh?" said Galen. "Well, clearly if you were assigned to the third form as a ten-year old, they think that you are more intelligent than your age. But I also sense an unusual maturity in you Creedon. It's amazing how quickly you are adjusting to this new life after being uprooted from your home and your parents. It's also remarkable how you are submitting to your parents' strange request to come here, rather than complain about it."

"Of course, *we* think that you are special," said Helen, "and Miss Mariada is giving you advice that would be good for anyone. In a perfect world, we would all rejoice in each other's unique gifts, but this is not a perfect world. So we have to account for the foibles of our fellow human beings."

"I do think," said Galen, "that there is something magical, Creedon, about the way you showed up on our doorstep in the middle of a stormy night. That sort of thing doesn't just happen."

"Indeed," said Helen. "And now I think it's time for dessert."

After a sweet lemony-tasting cake, and hot cocoa made with real cream, Creedon helped to wash the dishes and then he said good-night. Helen and Galen sat by the fire talking in low voices and wondering if legends ever actually come true.

5 KIDS WHO ARE DIFFERENT

Creedon was having a fitful dream. In the dream, the people of Almas became bears and started chasing him out of town. He reached into his pockets but had no candy to offer them. He woke with a start, just as the bears were about to catch him.

It was still night but Creedon was wide awake. He looked around him, disoriented for a moment. Where was he? Then he looked around the room and out the window and remembered where he was.

For the first time since he'd arrived in Almas, he felt a little lonely and afraid. He missed life in the palace with his parents and his friends, including the members of the Fairy Corps. At the palace, he had never had to worry about being a nail that stuck out, he was just who he was.

He pulled the covers around him tightly as it

was a bit cold. He wondered what his parents were doing. Then a light shone in the middle of the room. A small figure with wings appeared and bowed, saying, "Your Majesty, I apologize for the intrusion."

Creedon jumped out of bed and knelt to shake the figure's tiny hand. "Intrusion?" Creedon exclaimed, "Sir Gareth, you have no idea how glad I am to see you! Please 'intrude' any time."

Gareth was a senior officer in Their Majesties' Fairy Corps and had been an occasional tutor to Creedon in matters of history and government.

"Your Majesty," said the fairy, "I am to report back to the court on how things are faring for you here: your hosts, your school, the town and so on."

Creedon sat cross-legged on the floor while Gareth flew in mid-air, like a hummingbird, to be at eye-level with Creedon. With relish, Creedon quietly recounted everything that had transpired since he knocked on The Evergreen's door earlier that week (though now it seemed like ages ago). Creedon suspected that the High King and Queen already knew all of these details, but maybe they just wanted to hear how he was feeling. Or perhaps they just missed him.

Gareth listened patiently to Creedon without interrupting. When Creedon had finished, Gareth said, "The incident with the bear is concerning, especially so soon after you arrived in Almas. Did any of your friends notice when you put your hand up to stop the bear?"

"I don't think so," said Creedon, "I took a step backward so that they couldn't see it. They were focused on the bear and I did it quickly so that it was only a second or two."

Gareth nodded appreciatively, saying, "Well done, very well done, Your Highness. A time will come . . . but for now you are doing exactly what you should be doing. I suspect that the bear was sent by the Whisperer; you remember him, of course? The Whisperer convinced your parents to send you away, although they knew that his 'secret' plan was to destroy you. Yes, I'm sorry to say that he is capable of such depravity and more. But he will learn the hard way that Their Majesties cannot be manipulated or cheated."

"Gareth, I miss the palace so!" said the boy with longing. "The longer I'm here, the more warnings and cautions I get, including from you. In the palace I felt safe and secure, but here I feel like I've been sent into danger."

"Your feelings are natural, Your Highness," said Gareth. "But we know that the High King and Queen would not have sent you here unless it was for the best. We know from history that sometimes the best things are hard things, at least in the short term. Do not despair, you are exactly where you need to be. One day you will rule over this realm, including small fishing villages like this one. When that day comes, you will look back and recognize that *this* time was integral to preparing you for *that* time."

"Galen and Helen were asking what I should call them, and we agreed that I would call them Aunt and Uncle. Do you think that is ok with Mom and Dad?"

"Yes, quite appropriate," said Gareth. "Helen and Galen are to be your surrogate family in Triletus until the day that you are reunited with the High King and Queen."

"Oh, I wish that could be soon," said Creedon wistfully.

"It will not happen," said Gareth, "until sometime *after* your eighteenth birthday. But the waiting will be worth it."

"In the meantime," said Creedon, "what exactly am I to do here in Almas?"

"That's simple," said Gareth, "your task is to be a ten-year old boy. But also, you are to be a secret representative of your parents to this village. Look for ways to care for your future subjects. How can you be of use to Galen and Helen as they serve the village as doctors? How can you serve your classmates, the school and even the Council? I've been given no list of tasks for you; part of your training is to figure out what to do. But we all have high confidence that you will do well."

"And now," said Gareth, "it is time for you to go back to sleep. Do you have any message that you would like me to convey back to the palace?"

Creedon thought for a moment and then said, "Please tell the High King and Queen that I am very grateful for how they prepared my time here, especially for my hosts Galen and Helen and for my teacher Miss Mariada and my friend Charley. I miss my parents and love them; I very much look forward to seeing them when I can. I guess that's it. Oh, and please give my regards to the Fairy Corps!"

"To hear is to obey, Your Majesty," said Gareth, "good night and sweet dreams." Then he was gone.

Creedon thought that he was so wide awake now that there would be no point in trying to go back to sleep. But he lay down and a moment later he was fast asleep. This time he dreamt of a fun game of kickball. Some of the children in the field had disabilities: one was on crutches; another was blind and a third was missing an arm. But they were all smiling and laughing and no one seemed to care about the score.

When he awoke, the sunshine was bright through the window. Creedon was ready for the new day, or so he thought. After a quick breakfast with his hosts, Creedon said good-bye and started on his way to The Schoolhouse.

While walking to school, he met up with Charley, Nate, Paul and Jasper. Jasper was on his way to tell the Council about the bear incident. As the five of them walked together, Jasper said to Creedon, "I'm on my way to tell the Council about the bear, but there's one detail I can't seem to figure out. My boys can't explain why the bear suddenly stopped when it was headed straight for

Charley and his candy. Do you have any idea about that?"

Creedon put his head down as he thought through his response. "Well, sir" he said, "we were all standing very still and perhaps the bear sensed that we did not mean him any harm. Maybe he was a friendly bear?"

"Ok, yes, that's all my boys could think of. I suppose even bears can be friendly, but who knows what goes through their heads? Well, have a good day at school, Creedon."

"Thank you, Mr. Jasper."

The group reached a fork in the road where Jasper turned left and the boys went right.

Creedon continued on with Charley and his brothers, who were still talking about the bear and excited to tell their schoolmates about the incident. Creedon wished that they would talk about something – anything – else. But he realized that if he asked them *not* to talk about it, that would only make them suspicious of Creedon. After all, an encounter with a bear was a natural topic for conversation between children, especially in a sleepy fishing village like Almas.

As they walked, Creedon glanced around, eager for a conversation about something besides the bear. Looking behind them, he spotted a girl about his age who was apparently blind. The girl was holding onto the arm of a younger boy for direction. This younger boy did not have a left arm so the girl held onto his right arm. Creedon dropped back to walk next to them.

"Hi, I'm Creedon," he said.

"Hello," said the girl, "I'm Millie and this is Leo. We walk to school together because, well, I can't see where I'm going. Are you sure that you want to walk with *us*?"

"Of course, I do. Hi Millie and hi Leo," said Creedon, "I'm new in town."

"We know," said Leo shyly, "everyone is talking about you."

"Oh, great," thought Creedon with a silent groan, "just what I want!" But out loud he just said, "Oh, really?"

"Oh yes," said Leo. "We heard that your parents sent you here from another place far away and that you are staying with the doctors and that you are really smart."

Embarrassed, Creedon quickly said, "What classes are the two of you in?"

"I'm in the second form," said Millie, "and Leo is in the first form."

As she said this, they arrived at the steps to the front porch of The Schoolhouse. There was a group of several older kids standing on the porch and watching them arrive. As the trio walked up the steps, Creedon could feel the group's eyes focused upon him. As they reached the top of the steps, an older boy pulled Creedon aside. Millie and Leo moved on, correctly gauging that they were not welcome in this conversation.

"I know that you're new here, but why are you

walking with *them*?" The boy pointed at Millie and Leo for emphasis.

"You mean Millie and Leo?" Creedon said. "I just met them on the way to school. Is there a problem?"

"Didn't you notice that they are *different*?" said the boy, whose name was Stode.

"Yes, I did," said Creedon.

"Well, that's the problem."

"I'm sorry," said Creedon as kindly as possible, "but I still don't understand."

"Normal kids don't walk with abnormal kids; it's just not done."

"Why is that? It's not their fault that they have disabilities."

"Actually, it *is* their fault. Bad things only happen to bad people, so it's as simple as that."

Creedon was appalled to hear this philosophy, but he worked to keep calm. "Stode," he said, "I don't think life is as simple as that. Many times people can have a disability without it being their fault. But even if their disabilities were their 'fault,' wouldn't the disabilities be punishment enough? Why would we punish them further by shunning them?"

Stode was shocked. This was the first time someone had ever challenged his rationale. He gave up trying to convince Creedon and just gave him a shove saying, "Move along weirdo, we'll talk later. This conversation isn't over."

The school bell rang and kids rushed to their

classes, past watchful Andreas at his desk in the foyer.

"Welcome back, Creedon," Andreas said. Creedon appreciated the warmth of a friendly greeting after his hostile confrontation with Stode.

Creedon also relished having an assigned desk waiting for him in the upstairs third form classroom. It made him feel like he belonged. Miss Mariada greeted the class and began with a math exercise. Students took turns at the chalkboard working problems out by hand. Creedon guessed, correctly, that Miss Mariada intentionally gave him the easier problems so that he did not stand out. While he could not hide who he was, he was learning that that he could endeavor to only stand out when circumstances *forced* him to do so, as with the bear at the creek.

Math was followed by a session about local Almas history and government. Creedon was especially attentive because in the palace he had been tutored extensively about Triletus but not about this particular village.

Miss Mariada explained that the village Council was the highest authority in Almas, but that the Council was supposed to act within the constraints set down by the High King and Queen in their Early Edict. "What happens if the Council does not follow the Edict?" asked a girl in the front row.

"There may not be an immediate consequence," said the teacher, "but somehow the High King and Queen find a way for there to be consequences that bring the Council back into line. For example, ten years ago the Council said that people should not help the poor citizens in Almas, because the Council wanted to pressure the poor to leave town. The four people on the Council who had supported that rule each fell on hard times in the months that followed. The Council then revoked the rule, surmising that the High King and Queen had taken action to enforce the Early Edict, which commands that towns be sensitive to their poor citizenry."

"Ma'am," said Charley raising his hand, "why didn't the Council want poor people to live here?"

Miss Mariada paused to consider her response. "Charley," she said, "I think there were two reasons. The first was a fear that poverty is like a disease, so that being around someone who is poor could lead to contagion. The second reason was that certain people believe that all suffering is punishment; the result of people doing bad things and so getting what they deserve."

"Like the Council members who fell on hard times because they violated the Edict?"

"Yes, good," said the teacher. "That's precisely the problem – sometimes we *do* bring suffering upon ourselves, like when one of you doesn't do your homework and so I have to make you stay after class to do it in front of me. But even when we do cause our own suffering, there's a difference between the High King and Queen imposing extra discipline on a person (on top of that self-imposed suffering) and us trying to impose extra discipline on each other without knowing the full circumstances. Suffering is a complicated thing and I don't think we can fully understand the reasons that we ourselves suffer, much less someone else, without walking in their shoes."

A boy who was perpetually late in submitting his home-work said, "Miss Mariada, what about all the times that I don't do my home-work and you make me stay after class to do it. Maybe you don't know all the circumstances behind that!" The class giggled at this.

The teacher thought for a moment, and then said, "That's true, but the reason I have you stay after class is not to make you feel bad or even to punish you, but rather to help you keep up with the rest of the class. It's for your benefit. Does that make sense?"

The boy nodded begrudgingly, just as the school bell rang to announce the lunch hour.

"Ok," said Miss Mariada, "excellent discussion, I'll see you after lunch."

6 A SON OF HEALERS

At the lunch hour, Creedon sought out Millie and Leo. He found the two of them eating together alone at the end of a long, otherwise vacant table. Because the other lunch tables in The Schoolhouse dining room were full, it was clear that the other students were intentionally avoiding this pair of disabled students. With a little curiosity at Creedon's choice of lunchmates, Charley and his brothers gamely joined them.

As the six of them ate and talked, first and second formers walked by with looks of admiration at Millie and Leo. The older students rarely mixed with young formers and never with Millie and Leo, because of their disabilities. The "rule" Stode had articulated to Creedon reflected the way most students thought about it: kids with disabilities must have "done something bad" to deserve it so it was best to just steer clear of them.

Millie was initially a little tongue-tied to have new tablemates after years of sitting with Leo alone. But Leo had plenty to say and was seizing this fresh opportunity for conversation.

Nate asked Leo what had happened to his left arm (there was only a stub of an upper arm after his shoulder). Leo seemed unphased by the question: "I really don't know, Nate," he said, "I was born this way. The doctors just said this sometimes happens."

"Does it make it hard for you to do stuff?" said Charley.

"I'm not sure," said Leo as he thought about it. "Because I've always only had one arm, that's the only reality I've known. I'm sure things would be easier if I had two arms, but I've always lived this way so it doesn't really *feel* hard."

Now that the subject had been raised, Paul felt comfortable posing a similar question to Millie: "Millie, have you been blind all of your life?"

"No," said Millie, "I was able to see for the first few years. But when I turned four years old, I started to see strange colors. A few days later, I woke up and it was completely dark; I couldn't see anything, even in the daytime."

"It's funny, Millie," said Leo, "we've been friends for a long time but I never asked you when you became blind. Do *you* feel like your life is harder because of it?"

"Absolutely," said Millie. "But I don't often stop to think about it. My father left home shortly after I became blind; I think he just felt too guilty or uncomfortable about my blindness to be around me (even though it wasn't his fault that I lost my sight). So, it's just been my mother and me together at home since I was five years old. Mom knows that if she keeps things in the same place around the house, then it's easier for me to know how to get around and do things on my own, even help clean and cook."

"You cook," said Creedon, "really?"

"Oh yes," said Millie. "I'm not a *great* cook but it's fun to do. You would be amazed at how much you can do without seeing when you have no alternative."

The conversation went on like this and the group was so engrossed that when the lunch bell rang, they all jumped in startlement, and then laughed at themselves for jumping.

Creedon said, "Thanks Millie and Leo for letting us sit with you."

"Any time," said Leo with sincere gratitude. "This is the first time anyone at school has ever sat with us at lunchtime."

As Charley and Creedon walked up the stairs to their classroom, Stode sidled up behind them.

"Creedon," he said, "this has to stop. And Charley – you should know better."

Creedon turned around on the stairs and looked Stode in the eye. He said, "Stode — Millie and Leo are no less important than you or me. Some day *you* could wake up blind, or *you* could lose an arm.

How would you want people to treat you then? Why don't you sit with us at lunch tomorrow and get a new perspective?"

Stode gave a hollow laugh and brushed by them up the stairs.

"You're a brave guy," said Charley to Creedon. "Stode is a bully around here and he speaks for plenty of other kids and adults. You need to be careful."

As they reached the top of the staircase, Creedon said, "I understand what other people think, but does Stode speak for you, Charley?"

Charley hesitated for a long moment before saying, "No, he doesn't, pal. Come on, we're late for class."

Miss Mariada did not chide the two of them for being late. She had seen the scene in the lunch room and the start of the confrontation on the staircase. She reasoned that Creedon would experience enough unfair chiding from others.

"Let's get started with science," she said brightly. As she began to write different classifications of animal life on the chalkboard, Creedon could not help thinking about the warnings from Stode and Charley.

"How did simple kindness become dangerous?" he wondered silently. "Something is wrong here."

After school, Creedon joined the same group as the day before to play kickball. As Millie and Leo filed out of The Schoolhouse, Creedon noticed and excused himself to talk to them.

"Do either of you play kickball?" he asked them.

Millie laughed, "I know my limits, but Leo if you want to play, I can come 'watch' the fun."

"Sure, I'll play," said Leo. As they walked over to the group playing kickball, Creedon saw a few of the other players grimace when they spotted Millie and Leo approaching their game.

Somehow Millie sensed their reactions and said loudly, "Don't worry folks, *I'm* not going to play; just Leo here." She took a seat in the grass where Leo guided her to.

Creedon announced, "Leo can be on our team." Someone came over and said softly to Creedon, "But Leo's only got one arm, how will he catch the ball?"

"I actually don't know whether he can," said Creedon, "but if he's open to playing, then I suspect that he knows his limits. In the worst case, we score less points than we would otherwise. It's just a friendly game for fun, right?"

The other kid shrugged and said, "Ok," and then said more loudly to the group: "The first team to score ten points, wins."

As it turned out, Leo had an unusual aptitude for catching with one arm. When the ball was kicked to him in the air, he would use his chest to absorb the impact and then use his one arm and hand to settle it. The ball was small enough that he could cradle-catch between his one shoulder and chin. Then he would let the ball drop to his hand in order to throw it.

As the lone spectator, Millie was able to discern from the sounds of play and children's audible reactions how things were going, so she cheered when Leo's team scored or got the other team "out." Leo's team was the first to score ten points so they won the game. Afterwards, several kids said they wanted Leo to play with them again. He beamed as he rejoined Millie and she took his arm to begin the walk home.

"Creedon!" called out Millie.

Creedon jogged over, and said, "Yes Millie, I'm here."

"I just wanted to say thank you, Creedon."

"What are you thanking me for?" Creedon asked.

"Thank you for . . . everything. You, sir, are a prince," she said with a smile.

Creedon blushed and stood there watching as she and Leo walked off.

"C'mon Creedon," said Nate, "are you up for more creek racing today?"

"Yes, of course," said Creedon, still watching Millie and Leo walk away. "But," he turned to Nate with a smile, "today I could do without any bears."

He and Nate walked together while Paul and Charley walked behind them. Creedon thought how grateful he was to have friends and somewhere to play. That morning, Galen and Helen had told him that, going forward, they would assume he was at Charley's house in the afternoons. So Creedon would not need to check with them every day unless he was going somewhere else after school.

As they walked up the main street, they saw Stode and a few other fifth formers playing with a large dog, or at least it *looked* like play from afar. As they got closer, they saw that the boys were actually throwing rocks at the dog (which Creedon thought looked like a golden retriever). The dog, inexplicably, was not running away; it just stood there barking at its tormentors. When Creedon's group came closer, Creedon realized why the dog didn't flee: one of the dog's front paws had been badly injured by a rock so that it could not run.

Creedon looked back at Charley as if to say, "What should we do?"

Charley looked back at him and shrugged as if to say, "Let's not make a scene here."

But Creedon stopped walking, so Charley and his brothers loyally stopped as well, all watching to see what would happen next.

Stode ran up to the angry dog, apparently to show his friends that he was bold. He reached out to pet the dog in a sarcastic way, when the dog snarled and bit Stode in the leg. All could see that Stode's leg began to bleed profusely. Stode fell down, howling in pain. His friends immediately ran away, scared that they would get in trouble.

Charley said, "Shouldn't we run too, Creedon? When Stode's parents come, they are going to blame us just for being here."

Creedon looked Charley in the eye and said,

"Charley, I feel like we need to do what we can for Stode and this dog. But I'll understand if you and your brothers decide not to stay and help."

Charley looked over at Nate and Paul and they instantly decided that they would stick with their new, strange friend.

"We're staying with you to help," Charley said for them all.

"Thanks guys," said Creedon. He took off his outer shirt and tore it into strips. Then he ran over to Stode and helped Stode to press a couple of the strips over Stode's leg wound as a bandage. Creedon then took two of the remaining strips and began to tie them firmly over the first ones already applied to Stode's leg, like a tourniquet, to slow the bleeding.

Creedon took the one remaining strip and walked over to the dog, who had calmed down but was still whimpering in pain. Creedon slowly put his hand in front of the dog's nose so that it could smell him.

"It's ok, I'm not going to hurt you," Creedon said softly to the dog. Creedon gently tied the strip over the dog's wounded paw.

Creedon picked up the dog and said to his friends, "Paul and Charlie – could you please help Stode to stand up? He can lean on you while he walks. We'll go to The Evergreen and see what Aunt Helen and Uncle Galen can do."

Nate said that he would run ahead so Galen and Helen knew they were coming.

As the group slowly made their way up the main street of Almas, a crowd of onlookers formed along the sides of the street. A man came over and, seeing Creedon struggle under the weight of the dog, asked if he could help. Creedon gladly handed the man the dog. The onlookers fell in behind them as they made their way to The Evergreen in this plodding, somber procession.

Nate reached The Evergreen first, breathless from sprinting. He found Galen and, once he had recovered his breath, told him that his brothers and Creedon were bringing a wounded boy and an injured dog to The Evergreen for treatment.

Galen grabbed Helen and the two of them ran out of the front door just in time to see the group arrive on their porch. The man holding the dog gently handed the dog to Galen. Helen directed that both the dog and Stode be brought into the house. None of the boys was still in the mood to play, so they sat on the porch to wait while the rest of the onlookers dispersed.

Helen came out and said, "Creedon, would you mind giving me a hand? I need you to hold the dog still while I dress its wound. Charley, Paul and Nate: you can go home now, I'm sure Jasper will be wondering where you are." Creedon sprang to his feet, grateful for something to do. After saying good-bye to his friends, he followed Helen into a room she used for medical procedures. She showed him how to hold the dog's legs down without hurting it.

"Creedon, you did a great job with triage here. How did you know what to do?" she asked.

"I must have picked it up somewhere," Creedon said modestly and vaguely. "Do you know how Stode is doing?"

"Galen is attending to him," she said, and then with a smile: "but I think that he'll live. How did all of this happen?"

Creedon replayed the scene in his mind, deciding what to disclose. "Well," he finally said, "maybe the simplest way to describe it is that a few kids' attempt at horseplay ended with bloodshed."

"That's a succinct way to describe it," she said skeptically while giving him a close look. "Stode has a reputation for being a bully, as does his father."

Creedon nodded noncommittally.

"This dog is a stray," Helen said, changing the subject. "If it belonged to someone in Almas we would know about it."

"Could he stay with us, at least until he's better?" Creedon asked.

"Actually, *he* is a *she*," said Helen. "We can talk to Galen about it over dinner, but Galen is just as much a softie as I am, so I suspect that I already know his answer. Speaking of Galen, why don't you knock on the door of his treatment room just to see if he needs anything."

As Creedon moved to leave the room, the dog lifted her head and followed his movements closely. Creedon walked across the hall and knocked on the door. "Come in," said Galen.

Creedon walked in just as Galen was handing Stode a pair of crutches. "You are very fortunate young man," Galen was saying, "the dog's teeth narrowly missed hitting your leg bone. I suggest that you not put full weight on that leg until the wounds heal a bit."

Stode looked at Creedon but didn't seem to know what to say. Creedon put a hand on Stode's shoulder and said, "I'm glad you're ok, Stode."

Stode nodded and muttered "Thanks" and hurried out as fast as he could on the crutches.

Galen and Creedon watched as Stode left the house and slowly navigated his crutches down the steps from the porch to the street.

Galen turned to Creedon and said, "What happened out there?" So Creedon told him what he had told Helen.

Galen gave him a look that said, "I know it's more complicated than that, but I'm not going to press for details." They went out to the porch to sit and watch the sun go down while Helen finished attending to the dog.

"Aunt Helen and I were going to ask you about the dog staying here for a while," said Creedon.

"Yes," said Galen wryly, "I guess I saw that coming."

"She says that it's a stray so it doesn't have anywhere else to go. Kind of like me, now that I think of it."

Galen put a hand on his shoulder. "Of course,

Creedon, the dog can stay. Things have gotten a lot more interesting since you showed up on our doorstep. Why don't we go get a head start on making dinner?"

So Creedon set the table while Galen cooked. Then Creedon went to see if Helen could use help situating the dog. Helen helped Creedon convert an empty corner of his bedroom into a makeshift doggie bed formed of soft blankets. The dog went to sleep as soon as they laid her down in the corner. They shut the door to give her quiet.

At the dinner table, Helen said, "I don't think we want to keep calling our newest member of the family 'that dog.' It's time for us to decide on a name, isn't it?"

Galen said, "Well, Creedon seems to have had a hand in the dog coming here. The man who carried the animal onto the porch said that Creedon carried the dog the first part of the way. So, Creedon, what name do you propose?"

Creedon thought for a moment. "What about calling the dog, 'Misha'? I don't know why, exactly, but she just looks like a Misha."

"Misha it is," said Helen. "I wonder what dogs eat. Galen: who do we know who has a dog?"

"John and Betty have dogs," said Galen. "Why don't we pay them a friendly visit tonight to see if they are receiving callers? We can introduce them to Creedon and get some canine care advice."

7 A FOE OF DEATH

After dinner and dessert, the three of them washed and dried the dishes together and then changed into fresh clothes (their earlier clothes were soiled from attending to Stode and Misha). Then they walked down the road to the home of John and Betty. It was a warm, starry night and they found the couple enjoying it on their front porch. Many other porches on the block were also full of folks visiting each other. Creedon would come to learn that if people in Almas were in a mood to "visit" or "receive callers" that they would just sit on their porch and wait for neighbors to come.

"Hello there," said Galen once they neared the porch, "may we come a-callin'?"

"Of course, come on up," said John, so the three of them walked past a small garden full of purple and blue flowers and up a few steps to find seats on the porch. Betty offered them cool

62

lemonade and chocolate biscuits, while Helen introduced them to Creedon.

"You all had quite a commotion at your place today I hear," said John.

"Oh yes," said Helen. "It was the first animal patient we've had in quite a while."

John pointed to Betty and said, "Betty saw the whole thing by the way. She was in the general store when that boy Stode and his buddies started throwing rocks at the dog for no apparent reason."

"We hadn't heard *that* part of the story," said Galen, looking over at Creedon quizzically. "Betty, what happened next?"

"The dog's paw was injured by the boys' rock throwing, so it couldn't run away," Betty said. "Stode decided that it would be a brave thing to tease the dog while it was unable to flee. So when he reached out to pet the dog, it big him in the leg, several times. Stode's friends were gone in an instant, but Creedon and his friends stayed to help. Creedon was quite a leader back there. He enlisted his friends to care for both Stode and the dog (though I felt more sympathy for the dog, myself) and then they brought them both to you."

"I see," said Helen, looking with pride at Creedon, whose head was down, hoping this discussion would end soon. "Our hero seems to not want the attention over there."

Sensing that Creedon's reaction was something more than embarrassment, Galen worked to change the subject. "It's not the first time that Stode has been an instigator," Galen said. "I would talk to his parents about his bullying if I didn't already know that such a confrontation would end with his father threatening a fistfight with me. The apple did not fall far from the tree." All four adults nodded; the temper of Stode's father was well known.

Betty and John asked polite questions about Creedon and how he had come to be staying with Galen and Helen. They had apparently already heard much of the story from others but still wanted to hear it directly from the source.

John said, "Creedon, you should know that Stode gets bullied at home, where his father does not tolerate any show of weakness. Stode then goes and takes his anger out on others, including that dog today. You'll need to be careful, he's bigger than you."

"Yes, sir," said Creedon, "I have already been warned."

"On the other hand," said Betty, "I sense that if anyone could have an impact for good on Stode, it's you, Creedon. You have maturity beyond your years."

"Thank you, ma'am."

As Creedon looked out over the neighborhood and saw other adults and children on porches in fellowship, he had more hope for Almas than he felt earlier in the day. As he smiled, a beam of moonlight reflected on his face like a spotlight. It gave Creedon an ethereal appearance. The adults all noticed it but Creedon was oblivious.

Creedon mentioned that he had met two children that day, Millie and Leo, and asked if any of the adults knew their families.

"Oh, yes," said Betty. "I know Millie and her mom, they live just a few blocks away. Millie is a sweet kid. Sometimes she walks around so confidently, even climbs trees, that I forget she's blind."

"I know about Leo," said Galen. "He's the first child to be born without an arm in Almas, as far as I know. When he was born that way, it really shook up his parents. Why do you ask about them, Creed?" (Galen was experimenting with "Creed" as a nickname for Creedon.)

"I'm just curious," said Creedon. "I enjoyed getting to know them today."

"Creed's also become friends with Jasper's boys, Charley and so on," said Helen.

"Oh yes," said John, "we heard about the bear sighting."

"Speaking of animals," said Galen, "I almost forgot the original reason we thought to come a-callin'. That injured dog who we treated today (we're calling her Misha) is recovering in our home. We know that you have several dogs," (one barked in the background, as if on cue), "so we are looking for dog parenting advice; what to feed Misha and so on."

"Do you know what type of dog Misha is?" said

John.

"She's a golden retriever, from what I could tell today," said Betty.

"Yep, a golden retriever," said Galen.

"Then follow me, Galen," said John, "I'll show you what we feed our two dogs and also offer tips for dog care." Galen and Creedon followed him to the backyard where the dogs were playing with John and Betty's two children, while the women stayed on the porch to talk.

"So, Helen," said Betty once the males were out of earshot, "you're kind of a mother now. How's that going?"

"Well," said Helen, "this is all very new for us and we are only two nights into the arrangement, but we already decided that Creedon would call us 'Aunt' and 'Uncle.' As you heard, Creedon says that he has parents who sent him to stay with us specifically and I believe him. But it's a funny thing, Betty: the night Creedon knocked on our door, I was really depressed. I had pretty much given up on ever having children and then here was this ten-year old boy on our doorstep."

"It sounds kind of magical," said Betty.

"Exactly," said Helen. "The Council agreed that we could host Creedon for thirty days and then we can re-evaluate the arrangement. Creedon says that his parents wanted him to live with us until he's eighteen years old but we have no way of confirming that."

"On the upside," said Betty, "you have missed

out on the early childhood diapers and the crying in the middle of the night."

"I would be lying if I told you that I didn't want to have the *whole* motherhood experience," said Helen, "but I'm grateful for what I can get. Here's an interesting thing – Creedon is different. In some ways he is more 'adult' than Galen and me. I'm telling you this because I trust you not to tell too many folks. Creedon is already concerned about being the 'nail that sticks out' around here."

Betty nodded. She understood.

"So," Helen continued, "not only is this an unusual 'mothering' situation, but I sense that this boy has a special purpose; a purpose that Galen and I have to be very careful not to thwart."

"I hear you," said Betty. "But Creedon's parents would not have sent him to you if they didn't think that you were both up to the task. They know that you are not perfect, and probably know that you have not been parents before. So, I imagine that if we asked Creedon's parents what they expect from you, that they would say, 'Just do your best, don't worry about making mistakes, because you will.' The scary thing about parenting is that you often don't even realize when you have made a mistake until it's too late. Good parents can sometimes disagree on what good parenting even looks like, so there's an art to it as well."

By this time, John, Galen and Creedon returned to the porch. "Thanks to John, we are now fully equipped to care for a dog," said Galen jokingly.

"We're here any time you want advice," said John. "And whenever you want Misha to have a playtime, feel free to bring her over. Our dogs will be thrilled to have another dog to romp with."

Creedon stifled a yawn, as did a couple of the adults, and they decided it was time to call it a night.

"It was very nice to meet you, Creedon," said Betty as her husband nodded beside her. "Galen and Helen, please feel free to bring Creedon over any time, we're here on the porch most nights when it's nice out."

"Will do," said Galen as they waved good night.

As the three of them walked home, Creedon said, "Aunt and Uncle . . . should I have told you about the whole rock throwing episode? I didn't want to be 'telling on' Stode. I really do want to influence him for good."

Galen and Helen looked at each other, searching for an answer, and Galen spoke first, "To tell you the truth Creedon, I don't know. I'm beginning to understand how careful you'll need to be about your gifts. Helen, that's why I tried to change the subject when John and Betty were singing his praises. I know we're both proud of him (though I think his parents are really the ones to be proud!), but I think we are going to have to be cautious in how we talk about him. Other parents brag about their kids and a degree of exaggeration is expected. But we are going to have to work from the other direction, and try to minimize the attention he gets."

"Yes, I see," said Helen. "I'm sorry Creedon. I was trying to just give you well-earned positive attention but I think we'll just have to do that in private."

"It seems odd that you would feel like you need to apologize for saying nice things about me," said Creedon. "I'm sorry for how complicated it's going to be hosting me."

"Nonsense," said Galen as he mussed Creedon's hair, "you will not apologize to us for being special! I sense that there are great things in store for you, and it will be our privilege to act as surrogate parents for you while you are here. We'll all just have to figure this thing out as we go along. Ok?"

"Ok," said Creedon and Helen in unison as they entered The Evergreen and realized how exhausted they were. It had been a full day, so they fell asleep as soon as their heads hit their pillows. But before he went to sleep, Creedon gave Misha a friendly pat on the head in her corner of the room. She looked up and waved her injured paw at him. Then they both fell into a deep sleep.

As Creedon slept, the Whisperer appeared and hovered in the same spot where Gareth had hovered the night before. He crept close to Creedon's bed and began to whisper into his ear: "This town doesn't deserve you. They are cruel and selfish. You should just run away." Creedon's sleeping smile turned into a frown.

Misha woke up and saw the tiny figure of the Whisperer. She gave him a threatening snarl and bared her teeth at him. Startled, the Whisperer quickly disappeared. Misha dragged herself over to the bed and gently licked Creedon's hand as it draped over the side of the bed. Creedon's sleeping frown turned up into a smile.

Creedon dreamt that he was back in the main street, reliving the scene with Stode and the other boys throwing rocks at Misha. Things in the dream were true to life as the onlookers followed them up the street with Creedon (and then the helpful man) carrying Misha, and Stode limping with the help of Charley and his brother. At first the onlookers were cheering and supportive. But then the onlookers became bears. They picked up rocks and began throwing them at Creedon.

He woke up in a fright. Seeing Misha sleeping peacefully in the corner, Creedon calmed and fell back asleep, this time to a dreamless sleep.

8 THE TOWN AGAINST
THE BOY

The next morning, Creedon woke to sunshine through the window. The nightmare already seemed a distant memory. "It's a new day," he said to himself, "perhaps it will just be a normal one." But he could not shake a feeling of dread.

That day did turn out to be an uneventful one and so did the next one and the one after that. Thirty days after Creedon's arrival in Almas, the Council approved Galen and Helen becoming Creedon's official guardians. For a while after that, the days, weeks and months were mostly ordinary. But there were occasional incidents that caused Creedon to "stick out" in spite of his efforts not to.

The next really extraordinary incident happened four years after Creedon's arrival on The Evergreen's doorstep. Creedon was fourteen years old and in the fifth form – with the oldest students at The Schoolhouse. He, Galen and Helen had become a close family, and Misha (whose paw had long since recovered) was as much a member of the family as Creedon.

One afternoon after school, Creedon was walking with Charley while Nate and Paul trailed behind them. Ahead of them walked Millie and Leo.

It was a windy day with storm clouds threatening rain. As they walked up the main street, suddenly a very large tree gave way and began to fall directly where Millie and Leo were walking.

Creedon and Charley noticed it early enough to yell, "Watch out!" But, seconds later, the tree fell directly on top of Leo. Leo had looked up early enough to see the tree falling and he reacted quickly enough to push Millie out of the way. But Millie, being blind, didn't know what had happened.

The four other boys rushed forward to see the enormous tree laying on top of Leo's head and chest. They could not tell whether Leo was still alive. Creedon immediately started giving directions: "Nate, please take Millie home right now. And Paul, go tell Uncle Galen and Aunt Helen that we're on our way to them with Leo."

Nate escorted Millie down the street while she asked him what was going on and he tried to explain. But Paul didn't move. He just stared at

Creedon and said, "How are you going to move Leo? Ten men could not lift this tree off of him."

"We'll think of something," said Creedon, "just go, please."

"Ok," said Paul, incredulous but compliant, "I'm going."

Charley looked at Creedon inquiringly. Creedon put a hand on each of Charley's shoulders and said, "What I'm about to do you cannot tell anyone about, ever. Understood?"

Charley nodded and said, "What are you going to do, Creed?"

"I'm going to lift this tree up high enough for you to pull Leo out from under it," said Creedon.

Charley nodded. The past four years he had developed a sense that Creedon was different enough that he could do this, even though Charley didn't know *how* his friend would do it.

Creedon looked all around the vicinity to determine if anyone was watching. He saw no one. Charley grabbed Leo's arms and watched as Creedon grabbed onto the fallen tree trunk in the place where it was easiest for him to get a grip and a hold. Creedon then lifted, and the gigantic tree rose up. Charley was so shocked at the sight that Creedon had to yell, "Charley, now please!" to shake Charley out of the reverie.

Jolted back to his senses, Charley quickly pulled Leo out from under the tree. Creedon lowered the tree back to the ground, looking around as he did so to confirm that still no one was watching.

Now that Leo was free, Creedon knelt by his body to check if he was breathing. Leo was *not* breathing.

"Charley, I want you to turn around so that you do not see what happens next," said Creedon.

Charley knew to do exactly what Creedon said, so he turned around. Creedon put his hand on Leo's wounded head and quietly said, "Heal." Creedon put his hand over Leo's heart and said, "Beat." Then he put his hand over Leo's mouth and said, "Breathe."

Creedon then gently scooped Leo up into his arms and said, "Charley, you can turn around now. Let's take Leo to The Evergreen."

Charley turned around to see Leo with his eyes wide open and quietly crying.

Creedon once again looked around to check if anyone was watching them, but he saw no one. However, through the window of one of the nearby stores one person had seen the whole scene play out: Marina, the chief of the town's Council.

As Creedon walked to The Evergreen with Leo in his arms, he said, "Charley, please don't tell anyone what happened here. It could create a lot of trouble for me. Do you understand that?"

"Not really, Creedon," said Charley. "Wouldn't you be a hero?"

"Charley, have you ever heard it said that 'the nail that sticks out gets hammered down?'"

"Yes. Oh, ok, I get it. You have a special gift and people would be afraid of that or they'd want you to use it for the wrong purposes or they'd expect you to use it all the time for everyone or something else . . ."

"Exactly," said Creedon.

Before they reached The Evergreen – responding to the alert from Paul – Galen and Helen had raced out into the road to meet them half-way. Galen gently took Leo from Creedon's arms.

"He was hit by a tree that fell," said Creedon by way of explanation.

"You're very fortunate, young man," said Galen to Leo as he carried Leo inside, "does it hurt anywhere?"

As Galen and Helen disappeared inside the house, Charley and Creedon sat on the porch to wait, watching the rain fall. They sat silently for a moment and then Charley said, "Creedon, I have to ask you: how did you do that, back there? It looked to me like Leo was dead. I don't know how you were able to lift that gigantic tree, and I *really* don't know how you were able to, well, give Leo life again. I've never seen anything like that before. It's like the stuff you hear about in legends but don't really believe can happen in real life."

Creedon thought for a moment and then said, "Here's what I can tell you, Charley: I have special abilities. You might call it magic. As time goes on, I learn more about the extent of these abilities. But my parents warned me not to let people know about these abilities for the same reason I asked you not to tell people about what I did with the tree and Leo."

Charley nodded and said, "I get it. But it's really sad that we can't trust people enough for them to know. Think how much more good you could do."

"Yes, it is sad," said Creedon looking down at his hands. Nate and Paul joined them on the porch along with Leo's parents, Millie and her mother. Nate had earlier delivered Millie to her mother and sat with them for a bit while Millie's mother cried in relief about Millie escaping harm and while Millie worried about Leo. Paul relayed that, after delivering the message to Galen and Helen, he had raced to the home of Leo's parents to alert them that there had been an incident with Leo but that the doctors were treating him.

There was a shortage of chairs on the porch, so the boys stood while the adults and Millie sat. "I'll go check on Leo," said Creedon. He went inside and knocked on the examination room. "Come in," said Helen, and Creedon entered to see Helen and Galen sitting with Leo. Leo was sitting up and smiling, though still a little traumatized.

"Leo's parents and Millie and her mother are on the porch, so I thought I would see if I could give them an update on Leo," Creedon explained.

"It's quite amazing," said Galen, "but I don't find that Leo sustained any injuries. Leo, are you sure that you don't feel any pain anywhere? I don't see any bruising or cuts."

"No sir, I feel fine," said Leo.

"Could you just tell us one more time what happened?" said Helen.

"Well," said Leo, "one moment I was walking with Millie while the storm winds were picking up. Then the next moment I saw this tree falling toward us. I was able to push Millie out of the way, but I think the tree hit me and knocked me out. The next moment, I was awake and Creedon was carrying me to your house. I appreciate your looking at me, Dr. Galen and Dr. Helen, but I think that I am fine." He stood up and took a few steps to show them that he could.

"Well then, let's go out to show your parents and friends, I know that they are all concerned," said Helen. They let Leo lead the way out to the porch, and when Leo emerged there was a loud cheer from everyone gathered there. They all tried to give him a hug at the same time.

Upon request, Leo told them what he could remember of the tree falling. Nate and Paul had seen Leo lying under the tree so they had questions, but Charley gave them a sign that they should wait to talk about it later in private.

Leo's parents thanked all of the boys for their role in helping Leo that afternoon and Millie's mother and Millie gave Leo a special hug for his act of bravery in saving Millie. Leo's parents insisted on taking everyone out for ice cream on the main street downtown, including Helen and Galen.

As Leo guided Millie at the front of their

procession to ice cream, those following behind them were struck by how much Leo meant to Millie as a friend and a helper. How would her life have changed if Leo had not survived the tree's fall, they wondered?

On the way, Charley took his brothers aside and quietly explained that he could not talk about *how* Leo had gotten free from under the tree. He asked them to keep quiet about it. They agreed, even as they sensed that Creedon had something to do with it. Like Charley, over the years they had acquired a sense that Creedon had special gifts that he did not want people to know about.

At the ice cream place, called The Treathouse, the adults sat at one table while the youth sat at another. There was an initial shyness about how to treat Leo, as when you are around anyone who has been in harm's way but is then restored to you. But Leo easily broke through the awkwardness by laughing and joking and teasing the others. Once in a while, though, Leo would look quietly at Creedon and wonder what *exactly* had happened. Leo vaguely remembered having the tree on top of him, but, he reasoned, perhaps he had just imagined that in his traumatized state.

There were no more "nail sticking out" incidents for four years after the tree fall. Marina, the chief of the Council who had seen Creedon lift the tree off Leo and then bring him back to life, had decided that she would tell her fellow Council members but no one else. The Council agreed that keeping it secret seemed like the prudent thing to do for the time being.

Although Creedon had told Galen and Helen that he would be leaving town once he turned eighteen years old, none of them raised the subject during the intervening years. Galen and Helen didn't raise the subject because they hoped Creedon might forget, or perhaps change his mind and decide to stay with them even *after* reaching eighteen years of age. Creedon didn't raise the subject because he hoped to be able to stay with them as well. But he had a growing feeling, in the pit of his stomach, that events would put the decision out of his control.

The day of Creedon's eighteenth birthday, Galen and Helen invited Charley, Nate, Paul, Millie, Leo and other friends of Creedon's to celebrate in the backyard of The Evergreen. There they celebrated by playing games and eating cake and ice cream. Misha was everywhere at once: running around and barking in a friendly way at all the commotion as if she was somehow in charge.

The kids started playing a game similar to baseball or cricket. As they played, Millie sat in a chair on the side "watching" the proceedings. Nate hit the ball to Paul, and Paul fielded the ball and threw it to Leo. However, Paul threw the ball wide to the side of Leo's missing arm, so that Leo could not catch it. The ball was flying directly toward Millie's head.

Paul and others yelled at Millie to duck her head out of the way, but in all the commotion she only could make out her name being called. So, Millie leaned forward in her chair to try to hear them all better. She leaned right into the speeding ball so that it hit her directly in the forehead. Everyone heard the "crack" the ball made when it hit Millie's skull. She instantly slumped into the chair and then her body slid out of it limply to the ground.

Everyone, including Misha, went silent. Galen and Helen raced over to Millie. Galen took her pulse and Helen listened to see if Millie was breathing. They both shook their heads, signaling to everyone that Millie was dead.

People started to weep, Leo and Paul especially. They knelt beside Millie's body as if silently begging her to get up. Galen and Helen were frantic as they considered how to break this devastating news to Millie's mother, who wasn't there.

Charley looked at Creedon standing in the grass. Creedon looked back at him, knowing what he was thinking. There was no point in asking people to leave *this* time.

Creedon walked over to Millie's crumpled body. He asked Leo and Paul to move so that he could kneel down beside Millie. Creedon put his hands on both sides of her head and said simply, "Get up, Millie."

Millie bolted upright as if she had just awoken from a deep sleep.

"Is anyone there?" Millie said in a scared, small voice, because people were so quiet and she was still blind.

Suddenly there was a bedlam of reaction as everyone rushed over to see the revived Millie up close. As people quieted down while they gathered around her, Millie said, "What happened to me and why are you all so excited?"

All eyes turned to Creedon for his response. "Millie, the ball was accidentally thrown at your head," Creedon finally said after hesitating, "but you're ok now."

"Actually, Millie," said Leo, "you were dead and Creedon somehow brought you back to life."

Millie nodded. She reached up for Creedon's hand and he gave it to her. "Creedon," she said, "I don't know how I can ever thank you enough. You have already been such a friend, and now I guess I owe you my life." She gave his hand a squeeze and he smiled a tense smile before releasing her hand.

No one else knew what to say. Galen and Helen came and put their arms around Creedon, recognizing the sacrifice he had just made by publicly reviving Millie.

"Well," said Galen, looking to shift the attention from Creedon, "it's still Creedon's birthday, so shouldn't the festivities continue? Let's just try a different game."

The festivities did resume, but everyone looked at Creedon differently: some with awe, some with fear. Creedon heard two friends whispering, "If

Creedon can do *that*, why doesn't he heal Millie's blindness too? And what about all of the other people who need healing in Almas?"

For the first time, Galen and Helen fully realized why Creedon had been so cautious before. Now that people realized he had this special power, they would question why he didn't use it more often.

As people left the party, Galen and Helen asked them all not to tell others about what had happened. But they realized, with sinking hearts, that their guests would still talk about it. After witnessing such an amazing event, how could they not? Indeed, one of the youth present had a father on the Council and excitedly told him the moment he arrived home.

That father relayed this information to his fellow Council members at the next Council session, saying, "This kind of power could be so valuable for Almas; shouldn't we finally ask Creedon to use it more widely, now that he's eighteen?"

That evening, Creedon consulted with Galen and Helen over dinner because they anticipated just such a reaction from people.

"Creedon," said Galen, "now that folks know about your power, they will ask you to use it for them. For all of them. Your Aunt Helen and I are doctors but we don't understand how your power works, so we should probably talk about it. People will expect you to do things for them, but at the same time they will also fear you. They will assume that if you have the power to bring someone back to life, that you also have the power to destroy life."

Creedon nodded and said, "The magic is somehow connected to my parents. Now that I have turned eighteen, I can tell you that my parents are the High King Axel and Queen Gwyneth. This magic is ultimately under their control. I can sense when they are fueling me to heal someone, like today, but it is not something I can turn on or off at will. I can only heal when they empower the magic."

Galen and Helen nodded. "So, for example, that's why you could bring Millie back from death but not heal her blindness?" said Helen.

"That's right," said Creedon.

"Well, we understand," said Galen, "but I'm not sure that others will."

Even as he said it, there was a knock on the front door. Creedon rose to answer it and there stood Marina, the Council chief.

"Hello Creedon," she said, "I've come to speak with Galen and Helen, are they in?"

"They are, ma'am. Why don't you have a seat here by the fireplace and I'll go get them," said Creedon.

Creedon went into the kitchen and told Galen and Helen that the chief of the Council wished to speak with them.

"Creedon, you should come and join us," said

Galen, "I'm sure this concerns you."

As they greeted Marina, Helen mentioned that they would like Creedon to join them if that was ok.

"Certainly," Marina said, "since this involves him. Under the circumstances, I'll jump right into the reason that I'm here."

Marina shared that she had heard from a fellow Council member about what people were calling the Millie Miracle at Creedon's birthday party. She also disclosed that she had witnessed the incident four years ago involving Creedon, Leo and the fallen tree.

"I'm sure that you don't need me to tell you that Creedon is a treasure," said Marina. "The Council feels that it would be wise, for all concerned, if Almas officially recognized this and created a structure for the village to, uh, protect and utilize Creedon's special gift. The Council grasps that if word about his gift spreads beyond the village, that Almas might soon be mobbed by people from across the entire realm of Triletus seeking magical healing. Even within Almas, we will need to ensure that Creedon can live a normal life. We want to ensure that Creedon has time to rest and relax and do other things, but also time that he can dedicate to using his gift for the good of the village. Of course, we believe that Creedon should be compensated for using his gift; it would be unfair to expect otherwise and I'm sure that everyone would be eager to do so."

Galen said, "We truly appreciate the Council's thoughtfulness. We also have been reflecting on how Creedon's power will affect the way people treat him and will cause them to seek him out for help. But Creedon has just been explaining to us that the power that enabled him to do this 'Millie Miracle' is not something that he can simply turn on at will."

"Is that right?" said Marina. "Well, Creedon, could you help me to understand how your power works?"

Creedon gave Marina the same explanation he had given Galen and Helen at the dinner table.

"Let me get this straight," Marina said after hearing him out: "your parents are the High King and Queen of all realms?"

"Yes," said Creedon.

"They are the same parents who sent you to live here eight years ago?"

"Yes, ma'am. They told me that I could not disclose that until I reached eighteen years of age," said Creedon, "and even then, they advised that I be cautious about who I tell."

"Yes, I can imagine why," said Marina. She looked at Galen and Helen and said, "We have quite a quandary here. Do you have any ideas for how the Council should proceed?"

9 WHAT NOW?

Galen and Helen looked at Creedon, who was deep in thought as he considered Marina's question about what the Council should do about him. As they all thought in silence, there was a knock on the door. Galen went to see who was there. At the threshold were six men and four women.

Millie's mother was at the front of the group. She said, "I heard about how Creedon brought my Millie back to life today and I want to ask him to give her back her eyesight as well."

A man behind her said, "My boy Billy has a limp, could Creedon please heal him?"

Leo's parents were also there asking Galen if Creedon could restore Leo's arm.

Other adults were asking for healing, either for themselves or for their children. One man even asking if Creedon could bring his wife, deceased for several years, back to life.

Helen, Marina and Creedon heard the commotion and joined Galen at the door, although Creedon intentionally stayed out of sight.

"Folks," said Galen, "we are conferring right now with Marina to talk about what to do. Creedon does have special power, but we are learning that it's not as straight forward as you might think. Just as there are limits on what Helen and I can do with natural healing, there are limits on what Creedon can do with supernatural healing. Could you please let us talk this through with Marina and then we'll figure out what to do from there?"

There were begrudging "ok's" to this, but also evident impatience, even anger, as Galen closed the door.

"That group could quickly turn into an angry mob," said Marina as they returned to the living room. "As Council chief, I am accustomed to reading a crowd's mood and I don't see any answers we can give that will help. These folks are desperate, and telling them that Creedon can only heal *some* people but not others, without a compelling explanation, will just make them angry."

Creedon turned to Galen and Helen and said, "Aunt and Uncle, I hate to be the one to say this, but perhaps it is time for me to leave Almas."

Galen shook his head vigorously and looked at Marina, saying, "This is crazy! Helen and I have never been able to heal everyone, but suddenly Creedon does a couple of amazing things and people expect him to do it for *everyone*. How did Almas become a place that Creedon feels like he has to leave after bringing someone back to life?"

Helen gently patted Galen on the arm. "It really pains me to say it, dear, but I don't see a way around this. Didn't Creedon tell us when he arrived that he would need to leave Almas when he turned eighteen? His parents must have foreseen how things would go. They must have anticipated that he would be forced to leave whether he wants to or not."

Marina's head was bowed but then she raised it to say, "I am so sorry, folks. I wish I could say that other villages or towns will be different. But I think we are talking about simple human nature here. It's time for me to go, so that the three of you can talk it over on your own. Creedon: I will not say anything to anyone about your possible departure. But if you *do* make the decision to leave, on behalf of the Council (albeit unofficially) I am so very sorry. I wish things were different. I wish people were different; we seem to be our own worst enemies."

She let herself out, making her way through the crowd of people still standing on the porch, down the steps and out to a line that now extended into the street.

"Folks, please, let's give this family space tonight," Marina said to the crowd. "They've had a long day, and these are uncharted waters. They need to talk this over as a family. Please give them time, by going home for the night. Creedon is not going to be healing *anyone* tonight." Most of the people left, but a few stayed for a while in hopes that Marina was wrong, before they finally gave up and went home as well.

Meanwhile, Galen and Helen desperately tried to identify alternatives to Creedon departing Almas, but they could not think of one. That evening's crowd was evidence that word was spreading fast and expectations were rising just as swiftly.

Creedon finally said, "I think that I should leave early in the morning, while it's still dark."

Galen looked at Helen and said, "Are we really saying that this is Creedon's final night here? I can't believe we are saying that!" Helen had no response to this. Creedon stood up behind their chairs and put an arm around each of them.

"Thanks to both of you for eight wonderful years," Creedon said. "You took me in as a stranger but have cared for me as your son. My parents certainly knew what they were doing when they placed me on your doorstep. I will never forget you."

Misha wondered in, sensing the grave mood. She snuggled against Creedon's legs where he stood. Creedon stroked Misha's fur as he looked down at the tearful faces of his guardians.

"We will miss you terribly," said Helen.

"You filled a void in our lives," said Galen, "and you have probably taught us more than we ever taught you."

"What should we tell folks after you are gone?" asked Helen.

"Just tell them that I left," said Creedon. "I don't think you need to get into the reasons. You can tell folks, truthfully, that I didn't tell you where I was going. It's true because I don't know where I'm going myself."

Helen and Galen tried to give Creedon helpful advice for his travels, and then they said good-bye for the foreseeable future. Creedon said he wasn't sure how early in the morning that he would depart, so he asked them not to wake up early for more good-byes.

As Creedon lay down to sleep, he fondly took one last look around his room, including at Misha asleep in the corner. He realized that it might be a while before he slept in a bed again. He still did not know where he would go next. But after the excitement of the day, Creedon quickly fell asleep.

In the middle of the night, he woke with a start to a bright light in his room. He saw Gareth, but this time Gareth was joined by another fairy who seemed vaguely familiar. Gareth said, "Greetings your Majesty. I am joined, with regret, by the fairy Maddox who is called the Whisperer."

The Whisperer nodded. Creedon was already aware of him and his rebellion, having heard the Whisperer speak at court.

"Before you depart Almas," Gareth began, "The Whisperer convinced Their Majesties that he should have an opportunity to give his own, uh, *advice* to you, in addition to my own," said Gareth.

"But first I will say this: you have been faithful to your parents' mission for you here, and you have correctly concluded that it is time to go. Please do not be discouraged by the conditions that lead you to depart; your subjects are flawed and misled – often deceived by this Whisperer. But your time spent here will play an important part in your future reign over Triletus."

Gareth looked at the Whisperer to cede him the opportunity to speak. "Your Majesty," said the Whisperer, "I completely agree with Gareth that your time here has been well spent. I only disagree with him that it is time for you to depart. These people need to be shown that they don't deserve you; that they have only glimpsed a small part of your power. Stay and show them the full extent of your power. Destroy the impertinent and then you can stay as long as you want here with Galen, Helen, Misha and your friends. Millie and Leo will need you now more than ever, won't they?"

Creedon looked at Gareth again to see if he would offer a rebuttal but he did not. "It's up to you, Your Majesty," said Gareth, "I have made your parents' position clear and that's all I was authorized to do. You are to make up your own mind about the future."

Creedon nodded and said, "Thank you, Sir

Gareth. As for you, Whisperer, there are elements of truth in your words, but those elements are only designed to camouflage the falsity. My parents told me that I would only live here until I was eighteen, and that then I would leave. Were I to stay longer now, acting in disobedience, my relationships with Uncle Galen, Aunt Helen and my friends would all be tainted by that. It is time for me to go."

"Now that you have made that decision," said Gareth, "I am to advise that you leave town by the main gate. If you follow that road, you will come upon two fellow travelers who will be your helpful companions. Farewell, Your Majesty, and safe travels."

Gareth and the Whisperer disappeared at the same time. Creedon packed a backpack and, after taking a final look around his room, and patting the sleeping Misha on the head, he quietly left the room and walked out the front door of The Evergreen.

As he walked down the main street and saw the homes and stores of friends for one last time, he felt a twinge of sadness. But he also felt a lightness of being, that this was all for good in a mysterious way. As he walked out of the city gate of Almas, the sun was just beginning to show in the sky.

As he continued to walk, he spied on the side of the road a boy and a girl sitting expectantly. "Hello, fellow travelers," Creedon said to them.

"Are you Creedon?" said the boy.

"Indeed I am," said Creedon.

"Then we are here to help you," said the girl, quite earnestly.

10 HELP FOR THE JOURNEY

"**I**'m Aubrey," said the boy reaching out his hand to shake Creedon's.

"And I'm Olivia," said the girl, who did the same. "It's an honor to meet Your Majesty."

"Well met, fellow travelers," said Creedon. "Why don't we walk and talk, perhaps you could tell me a bit about yourselves and how you came to meet me here?"

"Of course," said Aubrey. "Olivia, you are probably better at remembering the details, would you do the honors?"

"Certainly," said Olivia. "Prince, we come from another world. We live in a country called America and that country is comprised of states. We live in the state of New York in a city called New York City." Olivia didn't bother Creedon with all of the geographic details, but in the interest of precision, I will mention that they lived in the part of New

York City called lower Manhattan. New York City has five sections, called boroughs, and Manhattan is the center borough. It's a long skinny island that runs north and south. In Manhattan you find City Hall and landmarks like Wall Street, Times Square and wonderful museums. Aubrey and Olivia lived in a downtown Manhattan neighborhood called Tribeca (short for "Triangle Below Canal Street").

"Aubrey and I," Olivia continued, "are schoolmates and friends. Yesterday was our last day before a new school year and we decided to take the Staten Island Ferry, because it's free. We were talking about how we felt like we hadn't had any kind of adventure the whole summer and yet school was upon us. While we were talking, a blonde woman with a ferry uniform approached us and asked us if we wanted a free voucher for cookies at the ferry's concession stand. Of course, we said 'yes.'

"When we took the voucher to the concessions stand, there was no one else around. The same blonde woman was working behind the counter. Her nametag read 'Cordelia.' When we handed her the voucher, she gave us each a package of cookies. Then she said, 'Aubrey and Olivia, are you serious about wanting an adventure?'

"Now, we don't know how Miss Cordelia knew that we had been wanting adventure, but we both were excited and said 'yes' immediately. She responded, 'Excellent. I am going to send you to a magical world called Triletus. Your mission will be to help the Crown Prince as he travels the realm, learning about his people so that he can one day rule them well. You are to be his friends and advisors in circumstances where the people you meet will not know that the Prince is royalty. Because time works differently in Triletus, when you return from that world to this one, you will return to this very spot at the very moment you depart. What do you say, are you still sure that you want to do this?'

"We both were still up for it, so Miss Cordelia handed each of us a little piece of purple cloth. She said, 'This is a treasure cut from the hem of the robes of the High King and Queen. Olivia, when you touch your cloth with your hand, it will enable you to hear and see anything if you set your mind on it. Aubrey, yours will provide an invisible shield around you and those in physical contact with you. Be careful in deciding who you tell about the cloths; I recommend that you disclose your treasure to as few people as possible. Now, if you are ready to be transported to Triletus, just bite into one of your cookies, each of you, at the same time. When you do that, you will find yourself sitting by the side of the road in Triletus. Wait by that road for a bit and you will see the Crown Prince walking your way.' We bit into our cookies, and not only were they the most delicious cookies we had ever tasted, but we were suddenly sitting by the side of this road. Then, up you walked, Creedon."

"I have to admit," said Aubrey, "that I didn't expect a prince to be dressed as a commoner. Have you been living in poverty?"

"Not exactly," said Creedon, "but I have dressed this way as a disguise. I don't want people to know that I am royalty, for now. Come to think of it, the two of you are dressed other worldly and will stick out like a sore thumb. The next chance we get, we will need to find you similar clothes. Please, just call me Creedon, both of you, as part of our blending in."

"Fair enough," said Aubrey. "So where are we headed now?"

"I don't know," said Creedon. "I think I'm just supposed to walk until we come to a place that feels like the place to stop. We may need to sleep outside for a while. Are the two of you up for camping even though you come from a big city?"

"Definitely!" said Olivia. "We were looking for a true adventure before the fall school term after all, and we have both been camping before. The weather here seems perfect for sleeping outdoors."

They walked along for a bit, getting to know each other as they ambled along. Creedon told them about being sent by his parents to Almas, and then being taken in by Galen and Helen. He described turning eighteen years old and then ultimately being forced to leave the town.

"How about you," said Creedon, "are the two of you siblings or do you have separate families in New York?"

"We're not related," said Olivia, "just good friends. We go to the same public school but we actually first met at a kids' camp several summers ago where we discovered that we both live in Tribeca. My father died when I was little, so it's just my mother, my little brother and me."

"I live with my parents and my older brother," said Aubrey. "But back to you, Creedon. When we get to the place where you decide that we should stop, do you know what you will do then?"

"Actually, I don't know that either," said Creedon. "But seeing as we need to eat and you will need new clothes, I guess I should look for a job. Since we'll be traveling together, we should anticipate that people will ask why the three of us are apparently homeless. When that happens, I think we should keep our explanations to a minimum, but we can truthfully say that we have no parents here and so are living on our own."

"Will someone force Olivia and me to attend school?" said Aubrey nervously, wondering if this odyssey could qualify as an adventure if it involved school.

"No worries, Aubrey," said Creedon grinning, "in Triletus it's not unusual for children to work for their parents on a farm or a fishing boat as they get older instead of going to school. Even in the big city-states, where school is technically required for all children, they don't enforce the 'school rule' unless kids are getting into trouble."

They walked silently for a while until they

reached a town. A sign by the road said, "Welcome to Halos, the City of Freedom."

"*Freedom*, that sounds promising," said Aubrey.

"Yes, we'll explore how this particular town defines it," said Creedon grimly. After Almas, he was feeling cautious.

As they followed the road in the direction of the center of town, they saw, on the right side of the road, a campsite. There men and women, and a surprising number of children, had tents and campfires and seemed to be "living rough."

"We might come back here tonight," said Creedon, "but let's continue on to look around town while it's still daylight." When they reached the town center, they saw shops and Creedon walked into one where the proprietor seemed friendly. Creedon explained to the woman that he was new in town and looking for work. The proprietor suggested that he go to see a builder named Tollen who worked from a site down the road.

"Tollen always seems to need more workers," she said.

"I will go see him then, thanks," Creedon said, tipping his cap to her. He rejoined Aubrey and Olivia outside.

"On to see Tollen the Builder," he told them. As the proprietor had described, Tollen the Builder worked from a desk outdoors under a canopy (a tent without walls). As Creedon approached the desk, with Aubrey and Olivia hanging back, one messenger was just departing from Toller's desk with a package in hand while another messenger arrived to deliver Tollen something else. Tollen opened the package before looking up to acknowledge Creedon's presence.

"Hello, stranger," Tollen said, "I haven't seen you around these parts before, have I?"

"No, sir," said Creedon. "I just arrived in town and am looking for work. Someone suggested that I see if you could use a worker. I'm dependable and strong and a fast learner."

Tollen nodded encouragingly: "Yes, you're in luck. I am just starting a new project for the Halos town Council – a meeting hall so that they don't have to sit outside when the weather is wet. Do you have any experience with construction?"

"No, sir," said Creedon, "but I'd like to learn."

"Good," said Tollen. "The older workers will like that you are not here to take one of their jobs. I can only pay you the wages of a rookie, but that's only a place to start, right?"

"Absolutely," said Creedon.

"Right, well then: bright and early tomorrow morning, be on the main street by the general store. The foreman will be there and he will walk you to your construction site. The foreman's name is Goodfellow, and he'll give you guidance along the way." Tollen stuck out his hand and Creedon shook it gratefully.

"Thank you, sir, you won't regret this," said Creedon.

Tollen looked behind Creedon and noticed the two younger children. "Are they with you?" he asked Creedon.

"We just met on the road," said Creedon. "None of us have family here so we are just traveling together."

"Uh-huh," said Tollen absent-mindedly as he resumed looking down at a blueprint of a future building. Without looking up again, Tollen said, "Tomorrow morning, main street, bright and early. Don't forget and don't be late."

Creedon waved good-bye and rejoined Aubrey and Olivia who had found a seat in the grass nearby. "Ok, I've got a job," he told them. "Why don't we walk around this place a bit more just to get our bearings."

As they roamed around the town, Creedon observed that, unlike Almas (which was a small fishing village), Halos was a larger town with buildings being constructed all over the place.

Most buildings that were under construction had a prominent sign that said, "Tollen the Builder," so it was clear that Tollen had plenty of business. After they had a good walk, they returned to the campground they had seen when they entered Halos.

As soon as they entered the camp, they were approached by an older woman dressed for the outdoors.

"My name is Beva," she said, "may I help you?"

Creedon said, "Yes, ma'am, we are wondering if

this campground is open to everyone? We are looking for a place to stay while we are in town. We don't have any money yet but I start my new job tomorrow with Tollen the Builder."

Beva nodded, "We have quite a few of his workers staying here. This land is owned by Tollen, and I work for him as the campsite manager. The cost for a family is twenty percent of your daily wages to stay here. We also can provide meals for ten percent of wages (she pointed to a nearby canopy with tables and an outdoor kitchen). We can also provide you with a good deal on clothing and rent for bedding and tents."

Aubrey spoke up, "This is probably not a fair question, Miss Beva, since you manage this place, but we're new here: do you know if there are any housing alternatives in Halos?"

Beva shook her head and said, "Feel free to ask around, but I think you'll find that until someone can afford to rent or buy a house in town that this camp is the best alternative. Tollen intentionally prices lodging at this camp low enough so that people can save up over time and buy their own homes."

Creedon said, "Do you we need to commit to staying here for a certain length of time? We're not sure how long we will be here."

Again, Beva shook her head. "No, that's another benefit of staying here. If you work for Tollen, you'll get paid by the day. If you decide to stay here, then I can work directly with Tollen's payroll person to have the costs deducted from your daily wages."

"Well, Aubrey and Olivia, what do you think?" Creedon asked. They both nodded so Creedon said, "Beva, thanks, we will stay here tonight, and I'll guess that we'll need to rent bedding and tents."

They walked with Beva to a storage building where she pulled out three tents and sleeping bags. Then she walked them over to a vacant square of land marked off with small flags at the corners.

"Here you go," she said, "I'll be nearby if you need help setting up the tents."

As Creedon and the children each set up their own tents, Aubrey started whistling. They were grateful to have found lodging so quickly upon arrival. Just as they finished setting up their tents, Beva rang the dinner bell. They followed the other campers to the meal canopy.

The food was much better than they had expected. They sat at a table with young men and women. They all introduced themselves and Creedon mentioned that he would start working for Tollen in the morning.

"Ah, yes, most of us work for him as well," said one young man. "Tollen's fine so long as you do not get on his bad side."

"How do you stay on his *good* side?" asked Olivia, concerned.

The campers looked at each other uncomfortably. "Well, uh, you basically do what he tells you to do and you don't make waves," said the man. "Tollen doesn't like surprises and he doesn't like competition."

Creedon and the children nodded, although they wondered exactly what this meant.

"What's it like living here in Halos?" asked Aubrey to change the subject.

"It's fine," said a woman. "Did you see the sign on your way in about freedom?"

The trio nodded.

"Well, freedom here basically means that people can do whatever they want to do," said the woman. "The problem is that there isn't much restriction on what people *can't* do. So, if you are powerful, then things are great. But if you're not powerful, you don't feel very free at all."

The trio nodded, though their faces made it clear they weren't fully comprehending.

"Here's another way of putting it," said a diner: "there's lot of freedom to do what you want if you have the power to do it, but not much freedom to prevent things from being done *to you*. For example, if Tollen decides not to pay our wages tomorrow, then they simply don't get paid. If we go to the Council for help, they will say we should work it out with Tollen. Or if someone hurts you for no good reason, the Council will say to work it out with that person and not to bother them."

"Don't worry," said another woman, "if this doesn't make sense to you now, it soon will."

The trio finished their meal and then walked to their tents to turn in. While walking, Creedon said to the children, "There's no reason for you two to get up early when I leave for work in the morning; feel free to sleep in and explore Halos a bit further or just relax and have fun. I'll see if they give me a lunch break from work to come see you at midday tomorrow but, if not, then I'll just plan to see you at dinner tomorrow night, ok?"

"Ok," said the children, "good night, Creedon." As Aubrey and Olivia each walked to their own tents, Aubrey said softly to Olivia, "So, this is how the Crown Prince of Triletus lives. It's not very glamorous."

"No," said Olivia, "but, as he told us, this is his training period and it will end someday. I certainly admire his hopeful attitude about it all. This is pretty much the exact *opposite* of life in a palace."

11 GOOD-BYE TO HALOS

Creedon stood in the town center, bright and early the next morning, and along with other men and women was led by Tollen to their worksite.

"You will be constructing a building for the town Council to meet in," Tollen said, "and that's quite an honor. This is your foreman, Goodfellow, who some of you have already met; he'll give you your marching orders. Good luck."

Tollen rushed off and Goodfellow addressed the group, describing their regular working hours. He explained that most days they would get a lunch break, depending on their progress. He then mingled, speaking to each of the workers individually to assess their skills and past experience. Then he divided them into groups and distributed tools and work assignments, with the more experienced workers deputized by Goodfellow to be deputy foremen or forewomen.

Once the work began, Creedon enjoyed working with a hammer to make roof trusses until Goodfellow tapped him on the shoulder.

"Son," Goodfellow said, "you're a great worker but you need to slow down. We get paid by the hour around here and there is no benefit to going so fast."

Creedon reluctantly nodded, remembering the camper's admonition from the night before not to "make waves." But the strain of constantly having to remind himself to slow down was far more taxing than working at a normal pace would have been for him.

After lunch when Creedon resumed work, the foreman tapped him on the shoulder again and said, "You've slowed the pace down, but I also need you to use less materials. This all costs money, you know."

Creedon said, as respectfully as he could muster, "But I've just been trying to make the roof as secure as possible in case of strong winds or bad weather."

Goodfellow shook his head. "Not a problem," he said, "the weather here is always temperate. But, in the worst case, if the roof falls apart, they'll need to hire us again to fix the roof. It's all about creating a steady stream of business for Tollen, my boy, you'll get the hang of it soon enough." Goodfellow walked away.

Creedon was able to abide by Goodfellow's restrictions for a few days, but finally he decided it just wasn't right. He resumed working at his normal pace and used the amount of materials he thought was prudent for the job. This time his deputy foreman tapped him on the shoulder and escorted him to the side where Goodfellow sat on a bucket. The deputy foreman took his place standing behind Goodfellow with arms folded.

"Son," said Goodfellow, "I've warned you, but you just can't seem to adjust. You're working too fast and using too much material. I'm beginning to wonder whether another warning will do you any good."

Creedon shook his head. "I'm sorry sir, I just can't do it. It feels wrong to work slower than I can and to not use the materials that a strong roof needs."

"Ok," said Goodfellow, "then I'm sorry that I'm going to have to fire you. Leave your tools with the deputy here. It's really too bad, you know: I need honest workers – just not *too* honest. If you ever can get your head around working my way, then feel free to come back and we'll try again."

Creedon nodded, sadly, and decided to try one last attempt at convincing his boss: "Is there any way that I could persuade you, sir, that what I'm doing is in your own best business interest? If you show that you get projects done quickly and with quality, then doesn't that make customers want to hire you in the future?"

"Nice try," said Goodfellow, "but I take my orders from Tollen, and *he* decides what is good

The Lost Boy of Triletus

for business. He's the biggest builder in this town and the other builders all play nice with him because he gives them the projects that he doesn't have time for. Good-bye, son, and good luck."

Dejected, Creedon walked back to the campsite in time for lunch. Over the meal he told Aubrey and Oliva about losing his job. He talked to a few other workers and they mentioned another builder who it might be worth Creedon speaking to.

After lunch, Creedon walked to speak to that builder, who hired him on the spot. But later that afternoon, as Creedon was working, the foreman tapped Creedon on the shoulder and told him that, unfortunately, he would *not* be able to employ him after all. Tollen had put the word out in Halos that Creedon should not be employed by *any* of the builders, unless they wanted Tollen to stop referring them business.

"But here's a thought:" said the foreman, "have you considered becoming a builder yourself? Please don't tell anyone I said this, but you seem to be a natural. The architects who create blueprints for Tollen don't like working for him, and if they found a reliable builder who would pay them a fair fee, they might finance you to get started."

The foreman named a few architects Creedon could speak to. Creedon thanked him and went directly to see them, one at a time. Each of the architects agreed to help him get started, provided that he did not tell Tollen their names. They were all afraid of retribution from Tollen.

So, that very day, Creedon became a builder. He called his business "The Royal Builders."

Word spread at the campground that Creedon was hiring and some of the campers left Tollen to work for him. Customers began to hire Creedon for construction projects because he was always honest with them and delivered what he promised.

Creedon continued to live at the campground with Aubrey and Olivia because the three of them saw no reason to live elsewhere. Beva even developed an arrangement with Creedon (which she did not tell Tollen about) so that people could live at the campground by paying out of their Royal Builders' wages. Aubrey and Olivia enjoyed being able to help Creedon with Royal Builders' projects.

After a few months, The Royal Builders was doing quite well. Once in a while a customer would be speaking to Creedon and say, "You have a royal bearing about you, has anyone ever told you that?" Creedon would nod and thank them but he would not prolong such conversations.

Tollen the Builder, however, was not pleased to learn that he was losing business to his former employee. Tollen began to investigate which architects were providing Creedon with blueprints. He sent someone to sneak into Creedon's tent during the day and thereby found the names of the architects on their drawings. This was dutifully reported back to an irate Tollen.

Tollen summoned these architects and

informed them that they would have to decide whether Creedon's business was more important than his own. So, the architects came, glumly, to the campground to discuss this with Creedon that evening.

"We're very sorry," said one. "We would much prefer to work with you rather than Tollen. But he is the biggest builder in town and we can't afford to work without his business."

Creedon nodded and said, "I understand. I'm sorry for the awkward position that this has put you in."

The most senior of the architects put a hand on Creedon's shoulder and said, "You could easily be bigger than Tollen in this town, but for the Council. Tollen bribes them to get business and encourage others to give him business, and I know that you won't do that. I just don't see a way forward for you unless you are willing to compromise."

Creedon glanced at Aubrey and Olivia, who looked like they were about to cry. It all seemed terribly unfair. Creedon turned to the architects and said, "I guess this is the end of The Royal Builders, at least for now. Feel free to tell Tollen this news if it will help you."

The architects nodded sadly. One said, "But Creedon, what will you do now?"

Creedon said, "I don't know, sir. I'll talk to Aubrey and Olivia about it. Good-night to you all, and thank you for coming to deliver the news to me personally, it was a pleasure to work with you."

Each architect shook Creedon's hand as they left, conveying their sincere regret at this turn of events.

That night at the campground supper, Creedon spoke to fellow campers. "Since I won't be building anymore, is there anything else that this town needs?" he asked.

Someone said, "What about doing laundry? People in this campground and even in town all wash their own clothes by hand. Many would pay someone to do that for them."

Creedon looked at Aubrey and Olivia and they nodded: sure, why not?

So, with Beva's permission, Creedon set up a table in the campground with a sign that read, "The Royal Laundry." Customers could have their dirty clothes picked up every week by Aubrey or Olivia. Creedon would do the washing and then Aubrey or Olivia would deliver the clean clothes back to the customers the next day.

Over time, as the list of customers grew, Creedon began to hire fellow campers to help. Even Tollen the Builder sent his clothes to The Royal Laundry because it did not conflict with his own business interests and he recognized that The Royal Laundry did honest and quality work.

For the laundry, Creedon and his workers would use buckets to scoop water out of the local river and then would wash clothes by the river using laundry soap. They would hang up the wet clothes on rope with clothes pins to dry in the sun.

One day one of the workers was walking down the stony bank of the river with a bucket to collect water when she tripped on a stone and fell headfirst into a rock. A fellow worker quickly checked for a pulse and said, "She's gone." Inexplicably, the workers all gathered together and carried the dead woman's body to Creedon. He was sitting at The Royal Laundry table in camp taking orders.

They placed the woman's body on the table in front of him without a word. "She died because she tripped and fell and hit her head on a rock," someone explained.

The woman's sister, a fellow worker, was weeping in despair. "Can't you do anything, sir?" she said to Creedon. "She is, or was, my best friend in all the world. She has three children who are at school right now. What will I tell them when they get home later today?"

Creedon sighed, stood up and said to the woman and the other workers: "What would you have me do?"

There was silence. If anyone had an expectation, they were afraid to say it out loud. Aubrey and Olivia were standing nearby, on break between deliveries, and they held their breaths, sensing that magic was in the air. Creedon placed his hands on the dead woman's head and said, "Live, and may your head be healed."

The woman sat up. The workers helped her get

down off the table. Her sister was sobbing with joy and took the revived woman into her arms in an embrace. The others stood in stunned silence for a moment until they began a jubilant cheer.

Creedon looked at the ten or so people standing around him and said, "If you value what just happened, please do not tell others about it. Ok?"

"Of course, boss," they said, and they returned to the river bank to continue their work.

Aubrey and Olivia huddled with Creedon, and Aubrey said, "Why did you not want them to tell other people? What you just did here was incredible!"

Creedon reminded them about his experience in Almas. "Remember that I finally had to leave that village because people expected me to be a healer-on-demand."

"But if you have this power, why *not* heal everyone who needs it?" asked Olivia. "You have such a gift!"

"Because *I* don't decide who can be healed," said Creedon. "I get a sense, from the High King and Queen themselves, when it's time to use magic. But when I don't have that sense, I simply can't do it. I learned in Almas that people get angry when I don't use my power as they desire."

"Well," said Aubrey, "while I *hope* that no one will tell what they saw you do here today, Creedon, I *fear* that someone will tell anyway. People talk."

Sure enough, even as they finished dinner and walked to their tents, there was already a line of five people outside of Creedon's tent who sought healing for ailments. One of them was a man born with only one leg, who walked on crutches. Creedon told two of the five people in line that he could help them, but gently told the remaining three of them that he could not.

"We will pay you whatever you ask," one of the latter said desperately.

"I'm very sorry," Creedon said, "but it is not a question of payment."

Aubrey and Olivia did their best to explain this reality to the disappointed townspeople just as Creedon had explained the situation to them. Two of the people accepted their explanation, but the man on crutches was still upset as he stomped away.

When Creedon awoke the next morning, there was a line of thirty people outside his tent. They all wanted healing. Creedon asked the children to tend to the laundry business while Creedon patiently spoke to each person in line, healing those he was able to heal and explaining to the rest that he was not able to heal them.

Two of those Creedon could not heal that morning were very angry and went directly to the town Council to complain. The chief of the Halos Council came to speak with Creedon. Creedon gave the chief the same explanation that he had given others.

"You could make so much money if you could only find a way to heal everyone," said the chief in a pleading voice.

"I'm sorry, but it is not a question of money," said Creedon. "I can only heal some folks, and when I do, it is not for payment."

"This is very sad," said the chief. "I don't know by what power you heal folks, but I do know people. I fear that this situation will quickly become untenable."

The chief was right. For a few days, the Council had security officers attempt to maintain order in the ever-growing line of citizens outside Creedon's tent, where he healed some and not others. But ultimately the police officers told the Council chief that they were losing control. They feared a mob would form. Indeed, that very evening, several disgruntled people attempted to beat Creedon with iron rods. Aubrey suddenly remembered his purple cloth, and he and Olivia took Creedon's hands so that an invisible barrier of protection surrounded them. After the would-be assailants hurt their own hands beating fruitlessly against the barrier, they shouted some curses and threats before they finally gave up and left.

Hearing of this, the Council chief reluctantly returned to Creedon's tent and said, "Creedon, I'm sorry to have been right about this, but you and the children are going to have to move on. Unless you can find a way to heal everyone who wants it, things are going to just get more violent. It's quite sad, I know: because some citizens won't get healed, now *no one* will get healed. We're not very civic-minded around here."

"I understand, chief, no hard feelings," said Creedon, shaking the chief's hand. "We will be gone by the morning."

12 A HOST IN SEPADOCIA

That evening was their final campground dinner. Creedon and the children did not tell most people that they were leaving Halos because they did not want anyone to try to stop them. After dinner, Creedon pulled aside a young married couple who he trusted and confided in them: "If you would like to take ownership of The Royal Laundry business, it's yours," said Creedon. "I think that you two could make a go of it."

They were very grateful and insisted on paying him.

"No need," said Creedon, "I've earned enough already. I know that you will carry on with integrity and diligence."

In the middle of the night, Creedon gently woke each of Aubrey and Olivia in their tents. They had packed their clothes and food the night before, so in minutes they were quietly walking out of the campground and then out of Halos. None of the trio paused to look back.

As they walked silently in the dark (waiting until out of earshot of Halos to begin conversing) Aubrey and Olivia wondered how Creedon could be so calm about being forced to depart a second town. The New Yorkers had each fumed in their tents while struggling to fall asleep the night before. It all just seemed so unfair. If only the people of Halos knew who they were forcing to leave their town in the middle of the night!

When they got far enough out of town to begin talking, and the sun started peeking over the horizon, the children asked Creedon where they were headed.

"I was thinking of Sepadocia," Creedon said. "Have you heard of it?"

Aubrey shook his head but Olivia said, "I think so. Someone working with us at the laundry mentioned that it's the largest city in Triletus – quite beautiful and accomplished."

"Splendid, I'm game," said Aubrey. "But Creedon, how did you decide to shift from a midsize town like Halos to the biggest city in the realm?"

"A gut feeling, mostly," said Creedon. "Then last night I had confirmation from a trusted advisor, a fairy named Gareth."

"Wow, a fairy!" Olivia exclaimed. "I've only read about fairies in, well, fairy tales."

"Where we come from," Aubrey explained to

Creedon, "a fairy tale refers to something like a legend; a made-up story."

"Interesting," said Creedon, "where *I* come from, a 'fairy tale' is a history of fairies, in the same way that Halos history would be a history of the town of Halos."

"Speaking of Halos, Creedon," said Aubrey, "I have to ask this because it's been bothering me: why didn't you decide to stay there and fight? Clearly you have magical gifts and I presume that if you can heal with magic then you could also use magic to protect yourself."

"That's a fair question," said Creedon smiling, "and the answer is the same as the one I gave for why I cannot heal everyone who asks. The magic only works if my parents activate it. My sense was that they did not want me to have that kind of fight in Halos. And, come to think of it, they sent the two of you, who protected me in Halos when people were trying to beat me! One day, not too far off, the time will come for me to fight. It's just not here yet."

"Do you ever wonder why that's the case?" said Olivia. "I mean, why you can fight later but not now?"

"I can only speculate," said Creedon. "As I told you when we first met, I was sent into Triletus to experience life as other Triletians do, in order to one day rule them well. My parents decide what experiences, including the use of magic, will prepare me for that day. They must have concluded, at least as to Halos, that 'flight today, fight tomorrow' was the best course."

The children accepted this, reluctantly.

"Speaking of magic," said Creedon, "I was impressed by how *you* were able to protect us yesterday, Aubrey."

Aubrey explained about the purple cloth from Cordelia. "Until that incident, I had forgotten about my own cloth," said Olivia, explaining the special ability her cloth provided. "I just don't know when I will have cause to use mine."

They arrived at a small port where a boat lay docked. Creedon spoke with the owner-captain and paid him passage for all three of them.

"It will be just a few hours ride to Sepadocia," Creedon explained to the children. With the gentle rocking and slight wind, all three of them fell asleep in cots on deck and did not awake until the captain shouted, "Ahoy!"

Rousing themselves, the trio stood up and looked to the oncoming beach – a mass of white sand. The boat was not able to land on shore, so they took off their shoes and waded through knee-length water to get there, waving good-bye to the captain.

When they reached the shore, they did not see anyone around. But they observed a well-worn path, and looking back at the boat as it receded into the distance, they saw the captain nodding and pointing toward the path. So they followed it.

It wasn't long before the city of Sepadocia came

into view. Although there were no walls around Sepadocia, there was a splendid gate of gold – the only official entrance in sight. Sepadocia looked perfectly round on the outside with an incline from the outer boundary to the elevated town center. You could see much of the city from the outside as if looking up a hill.

As in Almas and Halos, there were no cars or other motor vehicles, so it appeared that citizens walked everywhere. Buildings were of various shapes and sizes and colors but there were no skyscrapers like in New York. There was a pleasing mixture of nature – a park here and there, waterfalls, even a small valley. The hearts of Creedon and the children lifted as they embraced, after the turmoil of Halos, the opportunity for a fresh start in this garden city.

As they entered the gate, they could see the Sepadocia city-state Council in session, but its members paid them no notice. The trio continued past them onto the town square and decided to sit in the square's lush green grass until they could decide what to do next.

"Creedon," said Olivia, "does it bother you that this Council pays you no notice, even though one day you are to rule over them? Such indifference would certainly bother me."

Creedon thought about this and said, "Well, here's one reason it doesn't bother me, Olivia. If they *were* to pay me notice because they learned who I am, what kind of attention do you think they would give me? In your world, when someone meets someone in authority over them, what do they do or say?"

Aubrey said, "Hmmm, I suppose that they either tend to flatter the person, or complain about something they are doing or ask them for something they want."

Olivia added, "Of course, on a good day, someone might be friendly or honest; they might give sincere encouragement or criticism depending on what they thought the leader needed to hear."

Creedon nodded, "Quite right, and unfortunately, in this world at least, the good days for a leader are few and far between. The day will come when town Councils take notice of my arrival, but in the interim I am happy to enjoy the anonymity. One day I will take on the work and burden of being known, which is the day for which my parents seek to prepare me."

After a few moments of silence, Aubrey said, "Should we think about where we will stay tonight? I don't see any campgrounds like the one in Halos."

Creedon said, "Yes, let's walk around and see if we can find something."

As they walked through the streets, they came to a snug home with a sign that said, "The Redwood." In the front lawn there was an older woman working in the garden on her knees. As the trio approached, from her knees the woman said in a friendly voice, "Hello, I'm Agatha. Who are you?"

Creedon spoke for the trio: "We are travelers who just arrived in town. I'm Creedon and these are my friends, Olivia and Aubrey."

Agatha stood up and wiped her hands on her apron, shielding the sun from her eyes with her right hand. "What are your plans, travelers?"

"We actually don't have *specific* plans yet, ma'am," said Creedon. "We thought we would start by seeing if we are able to find work and lodging here."

"Well, why don't you join me for sandwiches and lemonade here on the porch," said Agatha with a tone that communicated command as much as invitation. "You three look famished."

The trio needed no convincing. They were relieved to drop their bags just inside the gate to the lawn, and then to take a seat around the table on the porch. Olivia went to help Agatha in the kitchen while Creedon and Aubrey helped to set the table on the porch.

"I don't think I ever fully appreciated hospitality until now," said Aubrey. "It's such an encouragement to be invited off the street like this. Miss Agatha is a gracious host."

"Indeed," said Creedon, "and more to her credit, she doesn't know who she's hosting."

"Speaking of that," said Aubrey in a low voice, "I've been wondering about the whole kerfuffle back in Halo. Let's say there's a similar incident here where someone is sick or injured. Will you heal them? Because it seems like that is the point when the unpleasantness begins. If that happens, I'm worried that we will have to leave this city for the same reasons that we three left Halos and that you left Almas earlier."

"Aubrey, I understand your concern," said Creedon. "But this pattern of being forced to leave towns is not one that I can avoid until my parents end it. This pattern is woven into their plan for me. So, it's not really a question of *whether* it will happen; only a question of *when* and *how*. I'm very sorry, I know that the constant turmoil makes me a difficult friend to travel with. I would understand if you and Olivia decided not to associate with me."

Aubrey said, "I'll talk to Olivia about it, but I expect that she and I have the same view: we were sent here specifically to support you during your travels *and* troubles. Being your friends is our primary reason for being sent into this world. To abandon you would be to abandon our purpose and our adventure."

Creedon nodded with visible relief, "Thank you, Aubrey, I truly am grateful for that."

Agatha and Olivia emerged with a plate piled high with sandwiches and a pitcher full of iced lemonade. The four of them sat around the table and Agatha watched with delight as her guests dug into the food with gusto. After the trio's eating pace slowed down, Agatha said, "So, travelers, what is your story?"

Without disclosing the most sensitive bits, Creedon recounted his arrival in Almas. When he got to the part about leaving Almas (he didn't say why) and meeting the children on the road, Olivia and Aubrey took turns describing how they were brought into Triletus from another world.

Agatha absorbed all of this placidly while she sipped her lemonade. She looked closely at Creedon's face and said, "You have the look of royalty about you, young man."

Creedon responded, "Thank you, ma'am."

"Clearly there is magic involved in your traveling between worlds," Agatha continued, looking at the children.

"How about you, Miss Agatha," said Olivia in an attempt to change the subject, "what is your story?"

"I was born in a small town, not unlike the village Creedon describes Almas to be," said Agatha. "I was the youngest of three sisters. Not long after my tenth birthday, my mother died of a mysterious disease. My father did his best to care for us but, as he grieved my mother's death, he could not cope with all of the pressure of caring for us on his own. So, one day he just left us. He walked out of the house one morning. I remember he said to each of us, 'I'm so sorry that I am failing you, but I cannot go on like this anymore. It's not your fault, it's mine.'

"As he walked out of the door, my sisters were too stunned to react. But I remember running after him and calling, 'Daddy, don't go, Daddy don't go!' But he was running faster than me and soon he was gone, out of sight. Forever.

"My oldest sister went and told our aunt (our father's sister) what had happened, and our aunt would dutifully come around once in a while to look in on us. But she had her own children and husband to look after. My oldest sister was eighteen years old at the time, and very quickly she became a mother figure to us. Even after she grew older and married and moved out of the house, she still felt responsible for my middle sister (then sixteen) and myself (then twelve). Well, we also grew older and my middle sister married as well. My two older sisters both felt responsible for me, but I decided that when I was older I would move here, to Sepadocia. I don't know why, exactly. My sisters and their husbands would talk about Sepadocia in reverent terms, as did others in our hometown. I decided, before getting tied down there, that I should see for myself what all the big city fuss was about.

"So, when I turned eighteen, I told my sisters that I wanted to visit Sepadocia in order to determine if I could have a future here. I didn't realize, at the time, how fortunate I was that they had a friend who lived here in Sepadocia with her family. That friend let me stay with her for a while when I first arrived in Sepadocia. Soon I was able to find work, and later I met my husband, Angus. We met when we were both trying out for the

Sepadocia squad for The Contest with Murta (a kind of athletic competition with each city's squad comprised of men and women). Neither of us qualified for the squad, but we found each other.

"Angus' parents left him this house when they passed away, and we have lived here for a decade now. But I have never forgotten the tender way that my sisters cared for me when my father left, and how our aunt graciously stepped in to help. I also have deep gratitude for the friend that let me stay with her when I first arrived in Sepadocia. Because of all the hospitality I have enjoyed from people in my life, I make a concerted effort to be hospitable to other folks."

Olivia said, "Well, Miss Agatha, we are very grateful for this lunch."

Aubrey was staring at "The Redwood" sign above the door to the house. "Did *you* decide to name this house The Redwood, or was it already named that when you moved in?" he asked.

"Angus and I came up with that name," said Agatha proudly. "Redwood trees are incredibly old and tall, and even though our home is snug, we wanted to communicate that we are proud of it and intend to be here for the long haul."

"We have redwood trees in our world as well," said Olivia. "I think they only grow naturally in the State of California."

"Miss Agatha," said Creedon, "is Mr. Angus, uh, still around?" He was trying to politely ask whether her husband was still alive.

"Oh yes, very much so," said Agatha. "Right now, he's out working, but he will be back tonight. He works for Sepadocia's Nature Department, looking after the various natural areas of our city (parks, streams and so on). But now, back to the three of you: what will you do and where will you stay in Sepadocia?"

The trio looked at each other, unsure of what to say. Finally Creedon said, "To be candid, ma'am, we don't know. Our 'plan' in coming here was just to walk around and see if an idea or opportunity presents itself."

"Splendid," said Agatha, "then your plan is working perfectly. You three shall stay here."

"That is very kind of you," said Creedon. "I'm sure that I speak for all three of us when I say that we are overwhelmed by your offer. Are you sure there is room for all three of us?"

"We have two spare rooms," Agatha responded. "Neither is large, but Olivia could use one and you and Aubrey could share the other."

"I hesitate to ask," said Creedon, "but we don't know how long we will be here in Sepadocia. How many days are you offering to let us stay in your home?"

"It is an open-ended invitation," said Agatha. "Angus and I were never able to have children, and we would enjoy having the three of you young people around. Angus and I already know each other well enough," she said with a grin, "so you will give us plenty of new things to talk about at meal times. I sense, Creedon, that you have a special purpose for being here and, well, that I'm *supposed* to host you to further that purpose. Good, so then it's settled."

13 MURTA IS CURIOUS

The sandwiches and lemonade had been devoured and the conversation naturally faded, so Creedon and Aubrey excused themselves to clear off the table and wash the dishes. Agatha went back to work in the front yard garden. Once the dishes were done, the trio of travelers retired to chairs in the charming garden patio in the backyard, to continue their planning.

"This is a wonderful place to stay, it's a boon!" said Aubrey. "Now we just need to decide what we're going to do next."

"Must we *do* anything?" asked Olivia. "We already have plenty of money saved up from Halos."

"Part of my training," said Creedon, "is to work like other people work, so I don't think it's a question of funds. We've tried building and laundry, so how about feeding people; opening a

131

restaurant?"

"That could be fun," said Olivia. "Though where we come from, I hear that running a restaurant can be a lot of work, and some eateries don't stay in business very long."

"A concise menu and a partnership with a reputable local farmer-supplier would be key," said Creedon.

"Now that you mention it," said Olivia, "when I was in the kitchen with Miss Agatha, she mentioned a large farm owned by a businessman named Osias. She said that he is trusted and well-respected."

"Excellent," said Creedon, "shall we go to meet him?"

The three of them walked around the side of the house to the front yard, where Agatha puttered amidst bright yellow orchids, giving them loving attention. Creedon mentioned their restaurant idea to Agatha and asked if she had any advice about how to broach the concept with Osias.

"Just be candid, my dear," Agatha said after a moment's reflection. "You're a good man and so is he, so I think you all will get along well." She gave them instructions for walking to Osias' farm and then they set out.

When the trio crossed into the sprawling farm's entrance, they quickly spied Osias' home. Agatha had told them it was called "The Oak" and the sign above the door confirmed this.

When Aubrey knocked, the assistant who

answered the door said that Osias was out in the cow barn and he pointed them in that direction.

"Is it ok for us to just show up and talk to Mr. Osias?" asked Aubrey anxiously, "I imagine he's a busy guy."

"It's fine," said the assistant, "we don't stand on ceremony here."

The farm was beautifully laid out, with everything tidy and friendly signs pointing the way. For Aubrey and Olivia, who had spent their entire lives in a large city, this farm was a special treat. It was a ten-minute walk from The Oak to the cow barn. When they arrived, they saw a man making notes on a piece of parchment as he leaned against the entrance to the barn.

"Mr. Osias, I presume," said Creedon.

"Speaking," said the man as he looked up with a warm expression.

"My name is Creedon, and these are my friends Aubrey and Olivia."

"It's nice to meet you all," said Osias, "what can I do for you?"

"We're new in town," said Creedon, "and we will be staying, at least for the near term, at The Redwood, with Agatha and Angus."

"Good folks," said Osias, "very hospitable."

"Yes, Agatha basically invited us in off the street, even though we were strangers," said Creedon. "Anyway, my friends and I were thinking of starting a restaurant in Sepadocia, and we came here to ask whether you would have an interest in being involved somehow. It could be just as our supplier, or perhaps more of a partnership if we are able to come to an understanding."

Osias paused for a moment and then said, "Has anyone ever told you that you have the look of royalty about you? I don't know what I mean by that exactly, since I've never seen royalty, but the impression is striking."

"It has been mentioned to me from time to time, sir," said Creedon with a glint in his eye but straight-faced.

"Apologies," said Osias catching himself, "now back to your proposal. I would like to get to know the three of you better, perhaps over dinner at The Oak tonight? I have a good feeling about you three, and Agatha is a good judge of character. But I would first like to hear your stories, if that's all right with you, before we talk business."

Creedon looked at the New Yorkers for their reaction and they nodded in the affirmative so, he responded, "That sounds great, we will be here tonight."

"Please invite Angus and Agatha as well, if you could," said Osias. "I haven't seen them for a while and it would be terrific to catch up with them."

Creedon gave him a thumbs up as he and the children departed.

"This seems almost too easy," said Olivia.

"Problems will come," said Creedon, "but we can enjoy the smoothness now." They walked back to The Redwood and conveyed Osias' dinner invitation to Agatha, who was still at work in the garden. Agatha said that she would join them for dinner and that she thought Angus would want to as well.

The trio retreated to the back lawn where they continued to formulate the details of their restaurant proposal for Osias. Creedon invited the children to give their ideas.

"It would be great if we could have it somewhere *on* Osias' farm estate," said Aubrey. "That location would reinforce that it's fresh food and it would feel a little more restful than in the busier areas of town. It would literally be 'farm-to-table' dining."

"Yes, and we could have fresh sunflowers from the farm every day on the tables," added Olivia, "and red and white checkered tablecloths and light blue walls, lots of light, so that it feels like a picnic inside."

Creedon nodded with a smile, encouraging their enthusiasm and said, "Perhaps we could call it 'The Royal Eatery.'"

"Quite so," said Aubrey. "We had The Royal Builders and then The Royal Laundry, so I guess The Royal Eatery would be the natural next step."

"It does seem like our business names have been laying a trail of breadcrumbs, so to speak," said Olivia slyly.

"If people only knew who was serving them!" said Aubrey.

"People will know soon enough," said Creedon

with a weary smile. Agatha came to fetch them for dinner. She was joined by Angus, so there were introductions all around before they headed out to the farm.

As they walked to Osias' farm for dinner, Creedon was deep in conversation with Angus about his nature work while the children chatted with Agatha. When they arrived at The Oak, Osias was already waiting at the door to greet them. But instead of leading them inside the house, Osias walked them to a tree grove on his property which had a pleasant clearing of grass in the middle. There they found a table set with a snow-white table cloth and candlelight. (The tree grove and Osias prove to be the subject of an interesting story you can read about in the second tale of Triletus.)

Although they had all just recently met each other, the atmosphere was that of old friends reuniting and bound by an unspoken understanding. The Sepadocians inquired about the children's world and vice-versa, and there was much friendly laughter. A young man and woman from the farm staff stood by and discreetly served and removed dishes as the meal progressed.

When the group started eating dessert, Osias grew more serious and said, "We were going to talk about starting a restaurant. After spending this time with you, I am certain that we should do it as partners. But we don't have anything called 'restaurants' here, so, tell me, is it like a pub?"

Creedon let the children talk first, and then he summed up their proposal for The Royal Eatery. Osias put his fingertips together like Sherlock Holmes and thought for a moment. Then his face lit up and he said, "I like, I like it a lot."

They talked through more details and then Osias walked them to a nearby building that was vacant. "Until tonight, I wasn't sure what to do with this facility, but now I think I do," said Osias. "Why don't you three come by tomorrow afternoon. I'll have some of my farm staff show up, and we'll see if we can get it ready to go."

The children cheered and Creedon shook Osias' hand vigorously in thanks.

As they said good-night to Osias and returned to The Redwood, the Whisperer was watching them from where he hovered in the lower sky. He did not like what he was hearing. His face crinkled in concentration as he plotted a response.

Back at The Redwood, Creedon, Olivia and Aubrey fell into a dreamless sleep when their heads hit their pillows. Their revived hope, the warm welcome of their hosts and the encouragement of meeting their new friend and partner, Osias, made the sleep all the sweeter.

The next morning, Angus and Agatha cooked them breakfast. Angus clearly enjoyed having the company, as Agatha had predicted. When the trio arrived at Osias' farm that afternoon and made their way to the future home of The Royal Eatery, they were shocked to discover that the building's interior had already been painted a light blue. There were tables with red-and-white checked table cloths and fresh sunflowers in vases. Above the entrance to the building there was a regal sign that proclaimed, "The Royal Eatery."

Osias walked up to them and said, "What do you think?"

Their amazed expressions said it all.

Olivia exclaimed, "It's just as I dreamed it would be!"

Aubrey said with elation, "I don't even know what work there is left for us to do."

Creedon said, "I suppose we need to come up with a menu and figure out the kitchen situation."

He and Osias huddled to discuss this while the children wandered inside and outside the restaurant, admiring it from every possible angle. When Creedon and Osias were finished conferring, they found the children and said, "We think we can open The Royal Eatery tomorrow for lunch," and the children cheered again.

Osias said, "One thing you can do today – right now in fact – is to spread the word around Sepadocia, so that people know that we are here."

So Creedon, Aubrey and Olivia made signs to put up in high-traffic parts of town, and then set about posting them.

Meanwhile, the Whisperer visited the only pub in Sepadocia and found the proprietor looking bored behind the counter. The Whisperer knew that the man had already seen a Royal Eatery advertisement. He whispered into the man's ear that he should be concerned about the new competing establishment on Osias' farm and that the food was suspect, as were the foreigners involved. The proprietor looked around to see if someone was talking to him, but, seeing no one, he lazily concluded that he was just remembering what someone had told him earlier. He set out to speak to the Council about his new concerns.

When the pub proprietor arrived, the Council paused their discussion (it was something tedious regarding zoning rules or some such) to give him time to present his concerns. After hearing him out, they said that they would send a representative to Osias' farm to investigate. The council representative happened to know Osias well, and so went to speak to him directly when he arrived at the farm. Osias explained who his restaurant partners (Creedon, Aubrey and Olivia) were and also that the restaurant had not even opened yet.

"It's strange that someone would be complaining about the food before we are even serving it," said Osias.

"Yes," said the representative. "The pub proprietor probably doesn't want competition at mealtimes for customers, but I 'smell' someone else behind the rumor. I'll tell the Council that there is no problem here, but if you hear anything else suspicious, please let me know."

When the trio returned from putting up signs

around Sepadocia, Osias filled them in on the pub owner's complaint. Creedon said, "This feels like the work of the Whisperer," and he explained who the Whisperer was.

Olivia said, "Would this be a good time for me to use the purple cloth?"

Creedon responded, "Yes, definitely."

So, Olivia held the cloth in her hand and set her mind on the Whisperer. Instantly she could see and hear everything he was doing on the other side of town. At that moment, the Whisperer was, unseen, buzzing doubts into the ear of the Council chief (a respected man named Tyree) about who these "strange visitors were, including a lost man with a cryptic past." The Whisperer was doing this even as the council representative was reporting back to the Council about his conversation with Osias.

When Osias heard Olivia convey this, he said, "Let's go, right now – there's no time to waste!" The four of them ran to the Council's meeting place by the city gate.

When they arrived at the Council's meeting place, they could see the Whisperer but, for a mysterious reason ("probably magic," asserted Olivia) the Council could not see the fairy. The chief, Tyree, was just starting to parrot the doubts fed to him by the Whisperer as if they were his own (not comprehending that they had been whispered to him by the Whisperer). However, Olivia continued to relay to her companions what the

Whisperer was saying in real time.

The Whisperer said quietly to Tyree, "Who are these new people and why are they here?"

Hearing Olivia relay this, Creedon immediately spoke up and said, "Distinguished Council Members, you may be wondering about me and my friends, so let us introduce ourselves to you," and they proceeded to do so.

The Whisperer then spoke into the chief's ear, "Why do we need another place to eat in Sepadocia if we have the pub?"

So Osias immediately spoke up and said, "Council members, you may be wondering why Sepadocia needs another place to eat if we already have the pub. That is akin to asking why we need more than one park or tree or, come to think of it, more than one member for this Council. It's the variety that makes our city the beautiful mosaic that it is. Only a small number of our citizens can fit into the pub at one time, so The Royal Eatery will just be one more option with a unique atmosphere and a rather different eating alternative to the pub."

The Whisperer discerned that Olivia could magically see and hear everything that he was saying. He glared at her and was about to utter a cursing spell when Creedon shot him a look. Recounting it later, the children were not sure how to describe Creedon's look exactly, but Aubrey said, "I would do anything in my power to not ever have Creedon give me that look. It was chilling."

The Whisperer held Creedon's gaze for only a moment before the fairy flinched and disappeared. The Council was soon won over, and accepted Osias' invitation to be their first guests for the next day's grand opening of The Royal Eatery.

In the days and weeks that followed, The Royal Eatery became *the* fun place to be in Sepadocia. The lines were so long that Osias and Creedon worked out a lottery system. People who wanted to eat there could apply in advance and be told exactly what day and time to arrive, so that citizens didn't have to wait in line.

For a while, Creedon and the children filled whatever service roles were needed in the restaurant, but over time they hired other people from the community to fill them. The trio still functioned as cooks and waiters and management – popping in once in a while to see how things were going – but their hires proved trustworthy and so the trio soon found that they had free time on their hands again.

"What shall we do now?" asked Creedon.

"As we have toured around, I have noticed that there are struggling neighborhoods," said Olivia.

"Yes, wouldn't it be great if we could do something to help?" said Aubrey.

They met with the Council to ask for their input. With the Council's blessing, the trio visited the poorest neighborhood in the city. In the center of that neighborhood was a large abandoned house that was falling apart. Creedon bought the house and paid people who did not have jobs to help renovate it. He hired someone else to manage the house and Creedon called it a 'Royal Place.' People could come to the Royal Place for food and clothing and even to stay for a while. If they were looking for work, the person in charge would help them find work.

Soon, people from other poor neighborhoods asked Creedon to establish their own Royal Places. Over time, with Osias' partnership, they were able to start a Royal Place in every poor neighborhood around Sepadocia.

The Council began regularly asking Creedon for advice about helping the poor, as Creedon was becoming well-versed in the different needs of the struggling neighborhoods. The Council was overjoyed to see depressed neighborhoods becoming prosperous, vibrant and hopeful. As Aubrey and Olivia were also becoming well known, needy children would come to them when they sought help and didn't know how to get it. Or when their parents were too embarrassed to ask Creedon directly. Occasionally, the trio would stay overnight in a Royal Place, but most nights they continued to sleep at The Redwood, having treasured suppers with Angus and Agatha.

Word about these developments traveled to Sepadocia's rival city-state, Murta. The Murta Council sent word to the Sepadocia Council, asking for someone to deliver an official report on what exactly was going on.

14 ALL GOOD THINGS

When the Sepadocia Council received the request from Murta for a report on the Royal Places, there was commotion and consternation. Relations between Murta and Sepadocia fluctuated over time (from frosty to contentious to friendly) but seemed to be amicable at the moment. So, the Council wanted to be as accommodating as possible.

But, the Council members asked each other, who should deliver the report to Murta and what should the report say, exactly? The Council did not feel comfortable taking credit for what these three new arrivals to their town were accomplishing. So, they decided to send Creedon's trio to Murta along with Osias, who was already well known to Murta, along with two representatives from the Council.

The evening before traveling to Murta (which was about a four hour walk) to deliver the report, Osias met with Creedon and the children at The

Oak to prepare.

As they sat around the table after supper, Aubrey said, "Creedon, perhaps this will be the time to tell folks who you really are."

Osias gave an inquisitive look and said, "What do you mean by that, Aubrey?"

Aubrey looked embarrassed, having forgotten that Osias didn't know of Creedon's royalty. Creedon patted Aubrey on the back and said, "That's all right, Aubrey, it's time for Osias to know. You can tell him."

Relieved, Aubrey said, "Osias: Creedon is His Majesty, the Crown Prince of Triletus. He is the only son of High King Axel and Queen Gwyneth."

Without a word, Osias stood up from his chair, dropped to a knee, and bowed his head, saying, "It's a privilege, Your Royal Highness."

Creedon responded, "Thank you for honoring me, Osias, it will not be forgotten. Please rise and take your seat."

The children noted that as Osias returned to his seat there were tears in his eyes.

Creedon said, "I have been puzzling over this question – of when to publicly reveal that I am the Crown Prince of Triletus. I have no doubt that Osias' reverent reaction will be the exception, rather than the rule. So, I will wait until tomorrow to decide. But, in the meantime, we can plan what to say to Murta about the Royal Places."

They each agreed to be prepared to speak about a different aspect of their activity in Sepadocia to establish the Royal Places and thereby serve impoverished neighborhoods.

That evening, as Creedon and Aubrey lay in their beds, Gareth appeared and hovered directly above Creedon's chest. Aubrey was fast asleep but Creedon was awake, so Gareth spoke softly, so as not to disturb Aubrey.

"Your Majesty," Gareth said, "I have a word from the High King and Queen."

"Yes, Sir Gareth, go on," said Creedon.

"They say that it's time," said Gareth.

"I understand," said Creedon. "I trust that they understand what this means . . ."

"Yes," said Gareth gravely, "they do. But they asked me to convey that they are proud of you, and that the darkness will give way to light if you persevere."

Gareth then went on to update Creedon on various goings-on back home. This cheered Creedon up – thinking of old friends and haunts. Then Gareth said farewell and disappeared.

The next morning, Osias, Creedon, Olivia and Aubrey walked with their two Sepadocia Council escorts to Murta. They chatted as they walked so that the four hours flew by. When they arrived at Murta's city gate, they were surprised to see it festooned with banners and a sign heralding their arrival. A woman with a green dress escorted them to the Murta Council space where that council's members were anxiously awaiting them.

The Sepadocia Council representatives made

introductions. Then Osias gave the first part of the group's report on Royal Places in Sepadocia, followed by Olivia and Aubrey. Creedon was the last to speak and, in closing his portion of the report, he asked if the Council had any questions.

"Yes," said one member. "What motivated the three of you, who are so new to Sepadocia, to create these Royal Places? In other words, why does it take newcomers to accomplish what long-standing citizens never did?"

Creedon looked down for a moment as he contemplated whether to take the plunge. He then looked up and said, "I was motivated by love for my subjects."

"Your *subjects*. Did I hear that right?" said the inquirer.

"Yes," said Creedon. "For I am the Crown Prince of Triletus, the only son and heir of High King Axel and Queen Gwyneth."

This elicited a collective gasp from everyone present, except Osias and the children.

"Sir," said the chief of the Murta Council, "that is an incredible claim. People have been sent to prison for falsely claiming less."

"Yes," said Creedon, "I am aware. I make the claim knowing that you are likely to reject it. But before you reject it out of hand, please consider this question: what evidence would you expect from the true Crown Prince in order to validate his claim?"

Osias spoke up, "Distinguished Council, when

I learned this last night, I had no qualms accepting the veracity of Creedon's claim myself. I would expect the true Crown Prince to be dedicated to serving his people and this man has done no less. His noble bearing, speech and wisdom also testify that he is who he claims to be."

Creedon nodded his grateful acknowledgment to Osias.

"Other leaders have faithfully served their people before, so that cannot be the *sole* test," said the chief of the Murta Council. The two Sepadocia Council members nodded their agreement.

Osias said, "You must decide for yourselves whether this man is who he claims to be. I certainly believe it."

"So do we," said Aubrey and Olivia who stood in support.

"But I suggest that you be quick in your thinking," said Osias.

"Oh, why is that?" said the Murta Council chief.

"Because, if this man truly is your Crown Prince, then you dishonor him with your skepticism and indifference. His parents, the High King and Queen, would not be pleased with their son receiving such a cold reception. Their Early Edict instructs that one day their son would reveal himself to us, and that we are expected to welcome him as our lawful ruler."

There was murmuring to acknowledge the wisdom of Osias' warning. The Murta Council chief finally stood and said, "Mr. Creedon, we greatly appreciate you and your companions coming here today. We do not dispute that you are an honorable man who has done much to serve your city. We can only hope to replicate a portion of what you have done in Sepadocia in our own city of Murta. We will seriously consider your claim of royalty and investigate it promptly, with all due diligence."

Creedon nodded, and the two Sepadocia Council representatives hastily bid farewell on behalf of the delegation. As the group of six walked back to Sepadocia, there was an awkward silence. The minds of the Sepadocia Council members were racing as they considered the implications of Creedon's royalty claim. The children silently fumed at Murta's lukewarm response to Creedon and wished that he would "use his magic" to put everyone in their place. Osias gave Creedon a friendly pat on the back but he did not know what to say. How could one adequately comfort a Crown Prince who was greeted by his subjects with indifference and skepticism rather than celebration?

When they returned to Sepadocia, they stopped at the Council so that the two members could report on how the Murta trip had gone. However, when the two members reached the part where Creedon identified himself as the Crown Prince, they asked him if he wanted to relate that part himself.

"Actually," said Osias, "I will do that if His

Majesty does not object?"

The Crown Prince nodded, so Osias said with a loud voice, "Ladies and gentlemen, it is my privilege to introduce to you the Crown Prince of Triletus – the sole son and heir of High King Axel and Queen Gwyneth. All hail His Majesty!"

He and the two children knelt and two small children (who had casually wondered in off the street) also knelt. But the rest of the adults just stared at Creedon in stunned silence. Creedon gestured for Osias and the children to stand up and then he addressed the Council.

"I apologize that I was not able to tell you earlier, and I recognize that it may take some time for you to evaluate this claim. My parents sent me, a ten-year old boy, to live in a fishing village so that I would experience life in the realm. At the age of eighteen, I was forced to leave that village and later a subsequent town because of the turmoil resulting from my use of magic to heal and help people. My travels have shown me aspects of the realm that are worthy of commendation, but also aspects that require serious royal attention. I understand that some of you will accept my claim while others will reject it."

"Sir," said Tyree (the Sepadocia Council chief), "we are very grateful for your service to this city. But what evidence can you give us to support your claim to royalty? Your claim has serious implications and it would be foolish for us to accept it without investigation."

Osias was about to say something in anger, but Creedon stopped him with a gentle hand to his shoulder. "You are quite right to inquire, Mr. Tyree" said Creedon, "what evidence would satisfy you?"

The Council huddled and spoke in low voices. Finally, Tyree broke the huddle and said, "Your question challenges us, and to be perfectly candid, at the moment we don't know. We will deliberate further and call you back when we are ready, if that sounds reasonable to you?"

Creedon nodded and motioned for Osias and the children to follow him in departing.

15 WORD SPREADS ABOUT
THE LOST MAN

Word spread around Sepadocia that Creedon, who someone dubbed the "Lost Man" because of his mysterious history, was claiming to be the Crown Prince of Triletus. This set off an intense debate among the citizenry.

Those who lived in neighborhoods with a Royal Place proved most likely to believe Creedon's claim. They appreciated the tangible help of the Royal Places but they also insisted on believing that an element of royal magic was what transformed their neighborhoods.

Angus and Agatha were dumbfounded when they heard that Creedon was the Crown Prince. Once they recovered from the shock, they kneeled before Creedon, saying, "Your Majesty, it is a privilege to be your hosts. We apologize that we are not able to provide you with the accommodations which befit a king."

He urged them to rise. "You took us in," he said, "before you knew that I was Crown Prince, and your kindness will not be forgotten."

Those most hostile to Creedon's claim tended to have a business interest at risk. For example, the jobs that Royal Places created were making it difficult for businesses to continue to pay low wages to poor workers. Some accused the Royal Places of encouraging education for those who "did not deserve it." Criminal enterprise was also suffering in Royal Place neighborhoods.

The Whisperer was active, flitting from one group to another, planting seeds of anger or suspicion or doubt. He managed to camouflage himself so that people never bothered to ask who had articulated the notion whispered into their ears. He knew that if people *wanted* to hear something in their heart of hearts, that they wouldn't care *who* had said it.

In the midst of the Whisperer's murmuring and maneuvering, Creedon and the children just continued steadily on with their work. One day, during their walk into a Royal Place neighborhood, Creedon and the children were met by a little girl. She intentionally stood directly in their path, so that they were forced to stop.

"Yes, little one?" said Olivia kneeling down to speak eye-to-eye.

"My name is Clara and my father is very sick," said the child, "could you please come." She was looking up directly at Creedon.

So Creedon also kneeled and said, "Dear heart, has a doctor been to see your father?"

"Yes, sir," said Clara, "but the doctor said there is no hope for Papa to recover. Papa said that you are our only hope. Our mother left us because she could not cope."

"I can make no promises," said Creedon, "but lead the way, child."

The trio had to walk at double-time in order to keep up with Clara as she ran home with the desperate urgency of young hope. She led them to a small ramshackle house. When they entered it, they could see a toddler listlessly playing with blocks and a baby sleeping in a basket on the floor in the main room.

"Clara must be their caregiver since they don't have their mother anymore," Olivia whispered to Aubrey sadly. Clara led them to the bedroom where her father lay on the bed with his eyes closed.

Creedon quickly leaned over the bed to hold the man's wrist to feel for a pulse, but he felt nothing. He also discerned that the man was not breathing. Creedon looked at Clara and in her eyes he saw desperation and fatigue. As gently as he could, he said, "My child, I fear that your father is dead."

Clara kneeled with her head bowed before Creedon and said, "But you will not leave him that way, will you, Your Majesty? We are your loyal subjects and, as you can see, we are in great need."

Aubrey and Olivia did not dare to breathe as they awaited Creedon's reaction. Creedon looked at Clara with compassion before he sighed and said, "No, I will not leave your father in this condition. But here, my child, come help me. Put your hands on his legs and I will put my hands on his arms. Aubrey and Olivia, please attend to Clara's siblings in the next room."

Once everyone had moved into position, Creedon said, "Clara, what is your father's name?"

Until now, Clara had been remarkably composed, perhaps because she concluded that she had no other option. But now that she had someone older to help and feel her burden, Clara began to sob uncontrollably – so much so that she could not even say her father's name. Creedon waited patiently until she was calm enough to say, "His name is Amos, your Majesty."

"Amos," Creedon repeated, "good." He looked down at the man's closed eyes and said, "Come back, Amos." For a moment, nothing happened. But then Amos' eyes fluttered. Then his eyes opened and he blinked several times. He raised himself up on his elbows and looked around. Creedon handed him a glass of water which Amos gulped down.

Amos said, "Clara, who is this gentleman?"

Clara began to speak but she began weeping again, this time tears of joy. She buried her head in her father's shoulder. Creedon and Amos waited patiently until Clara quieted. Eventually she lifted her head and said, "Father, this is the Crown Prince of Triletus. He brought you back to us. We are forever in his debt."

Amos rose from the bed and kneeled before Creedon. Clara joined him. "Your Majesty," said Amos, "how can we ever thank you?"

"Amos, you have already thanked me by acknowledging who I am. Both of you, please rise. Tonight, we would be honored to dine with your family at The Royal Eatery on Osias' farm. But for now, I imagine you have work to do. We will leave you to it."

As the three of them exited the bedroom, they found Olivia and Aubrey playing with the little ones in the next room. The toddler, named Terry, looked up, and was old enough to realize that Amos was healed. He shouted and wrapped his little arms tightly around Amos' legs until Amos lifted him up with a hearty laugh of love.

Creedon motioned for Aubrey and Olivia to quietly leave with him while the family rejoiced in each other's presence.

But when they were at the threshold, Clara raced and caught Creedon by the hand. "You are not the Lost Man, dear Prince," she said, "*we* are the ones who are lost. Or were lost. Thank you for giving our father back to us."

Creedon smiled and said, "Farewell Clara, you have been very brave. We will see you tonight."

Once outside, Olivia said, "Should we ask them not to tell people what just happened?"

Creedon shook his head. "There is no further need for discretion. Word will get out, if only from the doctor who earlier saw Amos at death's door. In any case, we are entering a new chapter when it's time for the truth to come forth."

"But you still won't be healing everyone, isn't that right?" said Aubrey.

"Correct," said Creedon. "So yes, there will be trouble, not that we need to go looking for it. Shall we have lunch with Agatha and Angus at The Redwood?"

Meanwhile, a group of citizens was gathering in Sepadocia's town square. It began as a quiet protest against "Disruption by the Lost Man" but the Whisperer fomented it into violence. "Down with the Lost Man!" they began to chant, "Down with the Pretender!" Angus was standing nearby when it started and he stayed just long enough to grasp the direction things were heading.

Agatha and Angus were on their porch anxiously waiting when the trio arrived. The couple ushered them inside, saying, "It's not safe for us to sit outside on the porch today."

Once inside The Redwood, Angus briefed them on the riot that was growing in the town square in reaction to Creedon.

"I'm hearing that the Council is divided about you, Creedon," said Angus, "but even those members who believe that you are royalty are not willing to stand up to the mob that has formed."

"So, what do we do?" asked Aubrey, distraught. "I can't believe it has come to this. The more Creedon serves and helps, the more people want to hurt him."

"Let's have lunch," said Creedon calmly, "and speak of other things. After we finish lunch, I will go to the town square and attempt to dialogue with these Sepadocians." He said this in a firm way that did not invite argument.

At the time, the children felt like it was "pretending" to speak of other things in the face of such danger. But looking back later, they realized that Creedon was simply refusing to allow the danger to monopolize their conversation; there was nothing more useful to be said on the subject.

Over lunch, Angus talked about his work for the Nature Department and Agatha described her morning's visit with a friend. Then, for the benefit of Agatha and Angus, Creedon invited the children to describe their encounter with Clara's family.

For dessert, Agatha brought out warm apple tarts with vanilla ice cream, which was devoured with gusto.

After dessert, Creedon rose to depart with Aubrey and Olivia. He invited Agatha and Angus to join them for dinner that evening at The Royal Eatery.

"Can't we come with you to the town square?" asked Agatha.

Creedon shook his head, saying, "No, this is something the three of us need to do alone."

"Creedon . . . I mean, Your Majesty," said Angus, "I fear that things will get violent if you go to the town square."

"Things will indeed get violent there," said Creedon, "but you need not fear; I promise that we *will* still dine with you tonight."

As he and the children walked toward the town square, Olivia used her purple cloth to see and hear the proceedings that they were approaching. The chants of "Down with the Lost Man, Down with the Pretender" had turned to "*Death* to the Lost Man, *Death* to the Pretender." When she conveyed this to Creedon, he nodded but did not slow his stride.

When they arrived at the town square, Creedon found a park bench on the periphery and stood upon it. Once the crowd realized that the object of their anger was present, they quieted down to hear what he would say.

"This mob is kind of like the dog that finally catches the bus and doesn't know what to do with it," said Olivia to Aubrey quietly.

"Citizens of Sepadocia," Creedon began, "I recently came in peace to your fair city along with my two young friends here. We came to see how we could serve you. We extend to you the right hand of friendship."

In response to this opening statement, there were a few jeers but the crowd was mostly respectful. The Council had arrived to monitor the proceedings and were standing off to the side, so as not to be seen to align themselves with the mob *or* with Creedon.

Olivia held her purple cloth and set her mind on the Whisperer. She could see him whispering into the ear of one of the crowd's instigators. The Whisperer was saying, "Who does this fella think he is, creating more problems than he solves?" Olivia conveyed this to Creedon.

Creedon looked straight to the back of the crowd where the Whisperer hovered, visible only to himself, Aubrey and Olivia. Creedon said loudly, "Whisperer, be gone."

The Whisperer looked up, shocked at being discovered. He opened his mouth to say something but realized that, constrained by a more powerful magic, he could not. Fuming, he disappeared.

The children assumed that Creedon would say something conciliatory to the crowd but they were wrong. "We do not apologize for serving this fair city," said Creedon. "We do not even apologize for how our service might interfere with your business or personal interests. There is an infrastructure of injustice in Sepadocia that must be gradually dismantled in order for there to be justice. But there will always be opportunity for those willing to sacrifice, in the short term, so that justice can rise in the long term."

"Who are *you* to tell us what to do?" someone shouted angrily from the crowd.

"I am the only son and heir of High King Axel

and Queen Gwyneth," Creedon responded.

"If that's true," someone else shouted, "then where is your army?" This roused the crowd to anger and they surrounded the bench upon which Creedon and the children stood.

The crowd picked up any projectiles, such as rocks or garbage, that they could get their hands upon and began to throw them at Creedon. But Aubrey was holding his purple cloth, so while he and Olivia were huddled with Creedon, they were shielded from it all. The projectiles just bounced off the invisible barrier and fell to the ground in a sad pile. Those rioting closest to the bench tried to attack them with their bare hands, but every attempt left the would-be assailant with bruised hands and resignation.

"If we can't hurt them, then we can at least destroy what they have built," someone shouted. "Down with the Royal Places!" This got a rousing response, but when the crowd looked around them, they saw that an army had quietly appeared and was surrounding them. The soldiers' armor and weapons gleamed and their countenance was calm and fearless.

The commander of the army made his way to the bench. Seeing his sword and grave countenance, the crowd gave him a wide berth. The commander knelt before Creedon and said (loud enough for all to hear), "Your Majesty, your parents sent us to ensure that all was well in Sepadocia for you as its future ruler."

Creedon nodded and said, "Thank you commander. Citizens of Sepadocia, is all well?"

Half of those in the crowd quietly crept away (the soldiers permitted this at a signal from Creedon), while the rest knelt before him. The full Council membership approached and knelt as well.

"For now, I'll say things are as well as can be expected," said Creedon dryly. "Commander, please report back to the High King and Queen that my subjects and I are just beginning to get acquainted. Time will tell how our relationship can evolve."

The commander nodded. He wished His Majesty had not permitted *anyone* to depart without kneeling, but that was His Majesty's decision to make. With a whistle, the commander summoned his troops and they filed out of the square as quietly as they had arrived.

That night, as he had promised, Creedon dined at The Royal Eatery with the New Yorkers, Agatha and Angus, and the family of Clara and Amos. By now, everyone in Sepadocia was talking about the events of the day: Amos being restored to life, the crowd's inability to harm Creedon and the mysterious army that appeared out of nowhere. So even those at the Prince's table could not help but feel a little shy around him. Aubrey and Olivia were the most at ease, having traveled with Creedon for a while. But even they, at times, found themselves tongue-tied in the presence of the magical prince.

Osias' arrival at their table helped to naturalize things. He seemed most comfortable interacting with Creedon, sensing the Crown Prince's need for a friend. The rest of the table enjoyed sitting back in their chairs and listening to the two discuss farming and government and art. Creedon kidded Osias about not being married and Osias said, "I just haven't met the right woman yet, Your Majesty."

Creedon gave a mysterious nod, which Olivia later claimed meant, "One day you will," but Aubrey said it was ridiculous to interpret a simple nod that way. You can read about what happened to Osias in the second tale of Triletus.

16 PLEASE LEAVE

Word about the recent events burst out beyond Sepadocia and into the wider realm of Triletus. Specifically, citizens heard that there was a "lost man" who claimed to be Triletus' Crown Prince and the son of the High King and Queen. The news reached even outlying areas like Halos and Almas, where reactions were as mixed as when Creedon had lived there.

In many places, people said, "Sepadocia is so fortunate to have him, I wish the Prince would live here in our town!" But many in Sepadocia had a different view of the situation altogether.

For the powerful show of force by the army of the High King and Queen obviously did not generate an upswell of welcome among those who had crept away; not even among all those had made a show of kneeling before Creedon.

More than a few of his opponents said,

"Creedon clearly has *some* power behind him with the army and all, but that doesn't make him our ruler."

Others said, "Even if he is the son of the High King and Queen, they haven't been seen or heard from in ages. So who are *they* to order us around now?"

But Creedon was not, in fact, giving Triletians orders. For example, he continued to honor the authority of the Sepadocia Council. What created trouble for Creedon with the Council was the news about his bringing Amos back to life and how citizens reacted to that news.

Because, by the next morning outside The Redwood, a long line had formed. In line were the sick, the blind, people with missing arms or legs and even two gurneys holding dead people, carried by their friends and loved ones.

Agatha, Angus, Creedon, Aubrey and Olivia looked out a window at the line of people and Angus finally said out loud what the rest of them were thinking: "What's to be done about this, Your Majesty?"

Creedon said, "Might we retreat to your backyard to deliberate?"

Angus and Agatha said, "Of course," so Creedon, Aubrey and Olivia went out to the backyard garden patio.

Once seated, Creedon thought for a moment and then he crafted a sign that read as follows:

Creedon is not a doctor, so he can only heal through magic when able to do so. This is not a question of money or merit. If you are unwilling to accept a "no" to your healing request then please do not stand in line.

Out of respect for our neighbors, please do not stand in line between sundown and sunset. Those still in line at sunset will be given the right to resume that place the next day.

"Aubrey and Olivia, would you be willing to take turns managing the line as it snakes around the side of the house into this backyard?" asked Creedon. "This is where I can receive people who come. On the other days, if the line ever shortens, you can help me manage traffic in the backyard. Angus and Agatha, you should feel free to go about your days as normally as you can. Things cannot continue this way for very long, but for now this is going to be my daily work as Prince."

For a while, things went smoothly. Creedon would heal some citizens, but not others. He would bring some citizens back to life, but not others. Aubrey and Olivia tried to figure out a way to predict those Creedon could help versus those he couldn't, but there was no apparent rhyme or reason – no discernible pattern. Creedon didn't heal more men than women, or more old than young or the other way around. Wealth didn't make a difference, and neither did temperament or how nicely someone asked, nor the nature of someone's problem. Occasionally someone in line would ask Olivia or Aubrey for advice about how to increase their chances of being healed. In response, the children would apologize and say that they had no advice to give; that the only course of action was to explain the problem to Creedon and then wait to hear his response.

One day, a wealthy woman brought her sick son and Creedon said that he would not be able to heal him. The woman threatened to complain to the Council. Creedon quietly pointed at the sign where it said, "If you are unwilling to accept a 'no' then please do not stand in line." She stomped off in a huff saying, "This isn't over!"

Further back in the line was the Council's legal expert, who had brought his wife, who was blind. Creedon said, with chagrin, that he would not be able to restore her sight. The man nodded but plainly was unhappy with the result.

So, the next morning, when the wealthy woman addressed the Council and complained about Creedon, the legal expert spoke up in support of her complaint.

Someone else on the Council said, "But doesn't Creedon warn people that he will only be able to heal some of them?"

"That's what he *says*," retorted the wealthy woman, "but I think he discriminates against people of means and power."

"Even if that's true," said another Council

member, "what can we do about it? This man appears to be the Crown Prince of our realm and he has the military might to back it up."

"That's true," said the legal expert, "but I don't think this has to turn into a fight. The Prince has already shown that he does not want to use force. I think it could be as simple as our politely asking him to leave in order to keep the peace."

In an attempt to change the direction of the discussion, Tyree spoke up: "Are we really talking about asking this man to leave? Think of all that he has done and is still doing to serve our city. While he doesn't heal *everyone*, he heals many people, every day. Are we really going to exile him because he doesn't do *everything* we ask of him? If that were the criteria for residence in Sepadocia, this Council would be exiled because we don't say 'yes' to every request we receive, either."

For a moment there was silence because the chief's logic was difficult to refute. However, someone finally said, "Creedon is a troublemaker," and someone else said, "We'll have a mob on our hands." So, ultimately, Tyree felt compelled to call for a vote: two-thirds of the Council voted to ask Creedon and the children from New York to leave Sepadocia. The chief reluctantly said he would deliver this message to Creedon in person.

At lunchtime, Tyree arrived at The Redwood. Creedon and the children were having lunch inside with Angus and Agatha while the people outside waited in line. The chief knocked on the door and

Aubrey answered it, ushering him in.

"Can we offer you lunch, Tyree?" asked Angus.

"No, thank you," said Tyree, "and you may not *want* me as a guest after you hear what I have to say."

They all stopped eating and looked up at him.

"I am reluctantly here to say," Tyree began, "that the Council has asked me to convey that it would like Creedon, Aubrey and Olivia to leave Sepadocia."

Angus was furious and slammed his hand down on the table in disgust. "That is the most ridiculous thing I have ever heard!" he exclaimed. "Who has done more for this city in so little time as they?"

The chief looked sadly at Angus and said, "You know as well as I do, Angus, that this is not a rational thing. Any more than that mob in the town square when the Royals' army came. We are long past the point of reason."

Agatha said, "Imagine how many other cities and towns in Triletus would *love* the privilege of housing their Crown Prince."

"Yes," said Tyree, "many think they would, at first. But I think His Majesty knows that, eventually, things will keep ending up this same way."

Creedon nodded. "Yes, this has happened before, and the only mysterious thing to me is why my parents have instructed me to keep going through it. But, nevertheless, here we are. Tyree, I bear you no hard feelings. It was kind of you to deliver the message personally and in this gentle manner."

The chief kneeled before Creedon and said, "Your Majesty, please have mercy on this city. You are not the Lost Man; we are the lost people. We did not deserve your time serving us in the city any more than you deserve to be asked to leave. It's evident to me that even without an army you could destroy us with a simple snap of your fingers."

Tyree rose and said, "Sire, do you know what you will do next?"

Creedon shook his head and said, "Do we have a deadline for our departure?"

Tyree said, "We didn't discuss that on the Council, but I think as long as you stop receiving people in the backyard now that we should give you three days. If one of you will take down the sign in the backyard, then I will be the one to tell the citizens in line to go home. Farewell for now, perhaps one day Sepadocians will feel differently than today. . ."

Olivia took it upon herself to trudge to the backyard and remove the sign. Tyree walked to different parts of the line and explained that Creedon was no longer permitted to receive anyone for healing. Although people in the line were disappointed, no one seemed very surprised. They knew of the animosity that had been floating around the city against Creedon and had only hoped that they might receive healing before the proverbial "other shoe" dropped.

Creedon and the children used that afternoon to plan how they would spend their final three days in Sepadocia. They decided to use the first day to say good-bye to people working in the various Royal Places. They would use the second day to announce their departure to The Royal Eatery staff and introduce Osias as the new sole owner. Then they would use the third and final day to rest and say good-bye to their other friends around Sepadocia.

"Creedon," said Aubrey once their planning session was over, "where will we go when we leave the city?"

"I don't know," said Creedon, "but if past is prologue, then I won't be told our destination until the night before we depart."

Sure enough, the destination was revealed that final night after dinner and a tearful farewell to Osias, Angus and Agatha. It happened after Aubrey was asleep in the bed on the other side of the room and Gareth appeared hovering over Creedon's chest where he lay.

"Greetings, Sir Gareth," said Creedon.

"Your Majesty," said Gareth bowing while hovering, "I'll give you one guess as to why I am here."

"To relay our next destination," said Creedon confidently. "Something tells me that it will not be another city-state like Sepadocia."

"Quite so, Your Majesty," smiled Gareth. "You are to proceed to the Plateau of Waiola, which is equidistant between Sepadocia and Murta."

"And await further instructions once we're there?" said Creedon.

"Indeed," said Gareth, "or when you arrive at Waiola it will become clear what you are to do."

When the sun rose the next morning over Sepadocia, Creedon and the two children were already walking out the city gate. They stopped and turned to take a final look back at the city.

Olivia said, "Creedon, do you know where we are going?"

Creedon nodded, "We are heading to the Plateau called Waiola. Yes, you'll recall that we passed it on our way to and from Murta. Agatha and Angus gave us the tents and bedding in our bags, and we should plan to live rough again for a while, if that's ok with the two of you."

As he looked down at them, Creedon was reminded that they were, after all, just children. He knelt down to look them straight in the eyes, saying, "You have been my loyal companions and friends. I do not take your service lightly. You have come through so many travails already, I do not assume that you are still up for more."

Aubrey and Olivia looked at each other and then Aubrey spoke for both of them: "Your Majesty, our time with you in Triletus has been the highlight of our lives. We asked for adventure and now we have it in spades. So, lead on, Sire, we are with you until it is time for us to go."

Creedon gripped them each by a shoulder to

show his affection and then stood up resolutely and led them on their sojourn to Waiola.

It was only a couple of hours' walk to Waiola, but it felt like a lonely sojourn under the circumstances. When they arrived at the plateau, the children's heart sank to realize that there were no other people in sight for miles around. They entered the red rocked plateau on the left side (from their perspective) and after walking up a naturally-occurring clay ramp to reach the flat top of the plateau, they set up camp close to the rim of the plateau. They set up three tents, one for each of them, and after getting organized, they scoured the area to look for firewood.

Creedon coordinated dinner and a campfire that evening. He taught them old campfire songs he'd learned in Almas, and they taught him a couple of songs from summer camp in their world. There was something about the act of singing that helped them to feel a little less alone under all the stars and the full moon. As they sat around the fire, feeling a little sleepy but not yet ready for bed, Cordelia appeared.

"Your Majesty," she said as she curtsied before Creedon. "Aubrey and Olivia, it has been a while since we last spoke on the Staten Island Ferry."

"Greetings, fair lady," said Creedon, and the children said, "Hello."

"I have been asked to convey to Your Majesty that your parents are very pleased and proud of you. To you, children, they asked me to convey that they will never forget your service to their son."

"Thank you, Miss Cordelia," said Olivia. "Does this mean that it is time for us to return to our world?"

"Almost child, but not yet," said Cordelia. "His Majesty still has a little more business here that requires your assistance. But when it is time, he will help you on your journey home. For now, I advise the three of you to enjoy this solitude tonight, because tomorrow you will begin to receive more visitors than you can count. Whether you want them to come or not! Good night, courageous ones, good night."

The trio was heartened by Cordelia's brief appearance and message. Aubrey said, "If we will have company tomorrow, do you think that means that people will come to *stay* here with us?"

"It's possible," said Creedon.

"Then," said Aubrey, "in the morning I suggest that we pick our preferred campsite on this plateau before it gets taken by the crowd of visitors."

The other two agreed with him, and they decided that the opposite side of the plateau, farthest from the entrance ramp, would be ideal. At that other end was a small canyon with a stream running through it that they could use for drinking water and washing.

17 PAYING THE PRICE

The next morning, as Cordelia had predicted, people began to arrive at the plateau. A lot of people. So many people were arriving that Aubrey stationed himself at the top of the entrance ramp and directed them where to set up camp. Because Aubrey spoke with confidence and authority, no one questioned that they should do what the boy said.

As people arrived, they introduced themselves to each other while setting up their tents. Some came from Sepadocia and some from Murta, but many also came from other smaller and more distant municipalities as well.

Aubrey assumed that everyone had made the journey to request healing, and there were a few with that purpose. But most citizens said they were there solely to support the Crown Prince.

For, by this time, word that Creedon was at Waiola had spread from Sepadocia to the outlying areas. Concerned about unrest, town councils had quickly acted to forbid their citizens from traveling to Waiola to associate with Creedon. But those edicts had the opposite of their intended effect. People kept coming and coming. They brought their children and aged parents. When the sun set that first afternoon and people finally stopped arriving for the night, there were already thousands of tents and campsites set up around Waiola.

With his directing duties finished for the night, Aubrey reported back to Creedon and Olivia, who had been receiving those who came for healing. They had also been circulating throughout the camp to greet people. In the midst of the meet-and-greet, they happened upon a trained herald with a trumpet who agreed to be at their disposal.

This was fortunate, because Creedon said, "I think we need to call a meeting tonight to welcome everyone."

So, after people had finished their evening meal, the herald blew the trumpet and people naturally moved toward the sound. Creedon and the children had marked out a large grassy area near the opposite end of the plateau, the size of a soccer (or football) field, so that people could sit around on three sides while the trio stood in the open area of the fourth side.

Once everyone was settled around the field,

Creedon welcomed them and thanked them for their presence. "As you can see," Creedon said, "I welcome you with humble accommodation rather than opulent splendor. But since you have come, here is how I think I can serve you best: for the next seven days I will teach you how to serve this realm. Then you will return to your cities and towns and seek their prosperity. That is the 'victory' I seek for my beloved Triletus."

For the next seven days, each morning, afternoon and evening the trumpet blew to announce the gathering. At each session, Creedon spoke between a half-hour and an hour, and then he took questions. There was complete silence while Creedon spoke, but not a silence of fear; more of joy and anticipation. People were anxious to hear his every word.

The people had arrived filled with indignation that their own cities and towns forbade them to come. But Creedon exhorted them to return home in a spirit of love and mercy.

On the seventh and final evening, before Creedon could begin to speak, the Whisperer appeared along with an army of armed creatures. None of the armed creatures were human beings; most were a combination of different animals (such as a creature with a jaguar's body and a goat's head). Creedon motioned for the startled citizens to stay calm.

"Greetings, Whisperer," he said warmly. The fairy intentionally made himself visible to the crowd on this occasion.

"Your Highness," said the tiny Whisperer, "I bring good tidings. We are here to ensure the entire realm acknowledges your royalty."

"I see," said Creedon, "and how do you propose to do that?"

"Through the judicious use of force, if necessary," said the Whisperer.

"I am surprised that *you* acknowledge my authority," said Creedon. "What might you expect in return?"

The Whisperer's tone turned hesitant. "Well, sir, there would need to be considerable power-sharing, so to speak. You would, of course, be the visible leader. I would stay more in the background and give quiet direction."

"I see," said Creedon, "then I respectfully decline your offer."

"Whether you accept my offer or not," snapped the Whisperer, dropping the pretense of deference, "you know, as well as I do, that the people of Triletus must pay a price for rejecting your authority. That is a price that your own parents have demanded be paid. Because the rejection is not just an insult to you – it is also an offense against them. I am within my rights, on your parents' behalf, to ensure that the price is paid."

If the Whisperer had said this the first night people had arrived on the plateau, they might have been excited at the prospect of vengeance upon those who rejected Creedon as royalty. But after sitting under the Crown Prince's training, they knew to sit in silence, sensing evil in this proposal.

"You have more than a little responsibility for the people's rejection of me," said Creedon, "but no matter; I acknowledge that they are culpable as well. However, as their Crown Prince, it is my responsibility to be the first into battle and the last to eat in a time of famine. It is my privilege to pay the price that they owe."

"Then you are more foolish than I believed," said the Whisperer, who was sincerely shocked. "As you know, the punishment for this – the most serious crime in the realm – is to be thrown into a circle of wolves. You will not be permitted to use your magic to protect yourself."

"Yes, I understand," said Creedon. The people murmured their protest, but Creedon silenced them with a gesture. The Whisperer's army formed a circle and permitted Creedon to enter it. Ten wolves appeared, snarling with teeth bared. Raw meat was scattered around Creedon to whet the wolves' appetite.

The wolves surrounded Creedon and warily circled him. Creedon sat down on the ground and put his hands out. One by one the wolves stopped snarling and approached to lick a hand. Each wolf then stationed itself in a circle around Creedon, facing outwards.

The Whisperer howled in rage. "No, no, no! This is not fair. You cannot use magic, Prince!"

"I am *not* using magic, Whisperer."

"Then why are you still alive?"

"Perhaps these wolves are wiser than you are," said Aubrey.

"But you still have not paid the price," said the Whisperer, ignoring Aubrey. "The people have betrayed the Royal Family, and there must be blood."

"I know," said Creedon. "So, come and finish it."

All of the citizens rose in surprise – they had thought the worst of it was over. Aubrey and Olivia opened their mouths as if to object, but Creedon shook his head to convey that they should not intervene.

At first the Whisperer did not believe Creedon meant it. But when he saw Creedon dismiss the wolves and kneel down, he understood that the Prince meant what he said.

The Whisperer directed the creatures in the front of his army to advance with swords drawn upon the Prince. This they did until they were looming directly over Creedon. Other creatures came in between the swordsmen and began to punch and kick him. Soon Creedon's body was broken and lay crumpled on the ground. He was barely breathing.

"You heard the man, finish it," the Whisperer hissed through gritted teeth. The swords came down and did their work. For a moment, there was silence. Then the Whisperer said, "Three cheers for justice!" and his army gave a great cheer as they began to march away. At first, they were going to leave Creedon's body where it lay, but at the last minute the Whisperer turned and said, "Take the body."

But Aubrey and Olivia were standing by the corpse and they said, "The body stays." A few of the soldiers tried to push them away but Aubrey was holding his purple cloth and the soldiers only received bruises for their troubles.

The Whisperer shrugged and said, "Never mind then, just leave it. Let's go."

Once the army was gone, men and women ran to grab bedsheets from their tents and they reverently covered Creedon's body with them.

"Why wouldn't he stop them?" said Olivia through tears. "He did not deserve any of that, and he could have stopped them in an instant."

The crowd murmured its confusion as well. Aubrey said loudly so that all could hear, "One thing I know, is that His Majesty has never led us wrong. He would not have allowed this to happen if there were another way. We shall bury his body in the morning."

As everyone began to leave for their tents, suddenly there was a bright light that shone on the covered body. A crackling thunder ripped the heavens.

Everyone turned back to look at the body. But it was gone. The bedsheets were still there but clung to the ground and there was now nothing underneath them.

"What now?" said Aubrey, speaking for the emotionally exhausted crowd.

"What now, indeed!" said a voice behind the children.

They turned and for a moment the children were disoriented. A light shone from the figure so that they had to shield their eyes and squint just to make it out.

"Do you not recognize me?" said the figure.

"Is it you, Your Majesty?" said Olivia, desperately but with hope.

"Yes, it is I," said Creedon.

"We can barely look at you," said Aubrey, "you're so bright."

"I'm afraid that can't be helped, but my glow will pass soon," said Creedon.

"All hail His Majesty, the Crown Prince of Triletus!" said someone in the crowd, and everyone, including the children, knelt before him.

"Please rise, loyal subjects," said Creedon, "for today continues the restoration of Triletus and you are to be my agents in that restoration.

"In the morning, you will return to your home cities and towns and share what you have learned here at Waiola. Some will believe you and others will not, but their reaction is not to be your concern. Seek the prosperity of your cities and towns; do what you can to serve them and thereby show my love for my people. *That* is my work for you. Tonight, we shall celebrate new beginnings!"

The musicians among them ran to grab their musical instruments and they began to play them while others danced. The Crown Prince snapped his fingers and table after table of food and wine appeared in the middle of the field under giant pavilions with chairs a-plenty. People began a midnight feast. Children ran around and created improvised games as they naturally do on such occasions. Aubrey and Olivia escorted Creedon from table to table, introducing him to many citizens who were too bashful to approach the still-radiant Prince on their own.

The revels ended a couple hours later through an unspoken agreement among everyone that it was time. After sleeping late the next morning, people began to depart the plateau. Although they had been together only a week, they felt a special bond with each other. Citizens wrote down each other's addresses and vowed to keep in touch. Over time, they would come to call themselves the "People of Waiola Week" and would have mini-reunions within their towns to relive the week's events.

While they would go on to live with great hope and joy, their fellow citizens back home were uneasy when they heard what had transpired during Waiola Week. Some wondered why the High King and Queen still didn't show themselves, or why the Crown Prince hadn't revealed himself earlier to the realm. They wondered whether he was indeed who he claimed to be.

Even those who heard accounts of Waiola Week, and believed them, felt like the realm was still 'in play,' as it were. They feared that someone like the Whisperer could still come along and take over, perish the thought. Others simply refused to believe that anything had happened at all. It was all legends and nonsense made up by people without Practical Work to do.

The People of Waiola Week would return to their cities and towns as quiet supporters of the Crown Prince. When Waiola Week came up in conversation, and someone asked them why the High King and Queen did not appear personally that week, they speculated that it was because the Royals' appearance would have been terrifying. So that's why the Royals had sent the Crown Prince as their personal representative.

"And," the People of Waiola Week would say, "the reason the Crown Prince is not often seen is because many people don't really *want* to see him. We Triletians seem to have a problem with authority, even when it is as good as the Crown Prince. One day he will rule openly, but for now, he only gives what leadership we are willing to receive."

That morning, as people filed off of the plateau, Creedon sat near the exit ramp with Aubrey and Olivia to watch as the citizens passed and wave good-bye.

"Something tells me that it's *our* turn to depart as well," said Olivia looking at Creedon with a sinking heart.

"I'm afraid that it is, Olivia," Creedon responded. "I will miss you both terribly."

"Before we leave," said Aubrey, "I have to ask you, Creedon, about everything that happened last night. Why did you let the Whisperer and his army kill you when the wolves refused to? How did you come back to life? What does it all mean?"

Creedon put a hand on his shoulder and on Olivia's and said, "This is part of the longer story of Triletus. Before things can be put to right, as they one day will, Their Majesties' justice had to be satisfied. The Whisperer thought he would finally remove me, but last night he sowed the seed of his own destruction. He no longer has a rightful claim over the people of Triletus."

"As for how I came back to life, well, the Whisperer was only given authority to kill me, not to keep me dead. My parents never gave him that authority, so here I am."

"I don't know what it will be like for us to go home," said Aubrey. "Things have seen so exciting here and we're just going back to boring elementary school in Tribeca."

"My family still has work for you to do when you go home," said Creedon. "You heard what I told the people here this week, and the same applies to you. You can look for ways to be agents of peace and protection and healing in your world."

"But I thought your family only rules over

Triletus," said Olivia.

"Not at all," said Creedon, "this is not our only realm. Here it has been easier for you to hear and understand, but in your own world the Whisperer clouds communications and thinking. Still, fear not: when we need to make ourselves known to you, you will understand."

He embraced both children and then said, "Are you ready?"

"Ready!" they responded in unison.

"Farewell, until we meet again," he said. Then he began to fade from their vision while the Staten Island ferry came into focus. Once again, they were standing by the concession stand, holding the same cookies they had tasted to be transported to Triletus. Miss Cordelia was smiling at them in her ferry uniform.

"Well now," she said, "I told you the cookies were good."

The children looked around to see if anyone was listening, but it was just the three of them.

"This is the exact instant that you left for your adventure," Cordelia assured them, "you have lost no time here." She saw the children eying the cookies and said, "The cookies are still good, but they *won't* take you back to Triletus."

"Will we ever return to Triletus?" asked Aubrey.

"It's difficult to say," said Cordelia, "but for now, you have work to do here. Your adventure was not without a purpose."

The ferry horn blew to announce their arrival at

the Staten Island terminal. The children looked at the windows toward the East River and when they looked back, the concession stand was closed and Cordelia was gone.

They sighed, and stayed on the ferry as it left the Staten Island terminal to return to the Manhattan terminal. They looked out the windows at the East River and Statute of Liberty, not talking much. When they disembarked, they took the scenic route back to Tribeca, by way of the Battery (past the SeaGlass Carousel) and they kept looking around them in wonder.

"Are we *really* back here? Did we *really* go through all of that with Creedon?" said Aubrey. "It seems so far away now."

He reached into his pocket and felt the purple cloth, holding it up to Olivia. She pulled hers out as well and showed it to him.

"I guess it really did happen," Aubrey said.

When they each arrived home that evening, their parents noticed a difference in the children. In fact, Olivia's mother called Aubrey's mother and said, "Did Aubrey report something unusual happening today?"

"Well," said Aubrey's mother, "he said that he and Olivia rode the Staten Island Ferry and had yummy cookies."

"That's what Olivia said," responded her mother. "She also said something about it being an adventure. But it seems like Olivia has matured five years in a single day. She is listening to me more than she ever did before. She's much more patient with her younger brother."

"Aubrey seems different too," said his mother, "he actually volunteered to wash the dishes tonight. He even asked *us* questions about our day."

"Well, whatever it was that happened," said Olivia's mother, "I am grateful; I just don't know who to thank. Let's get together soon – bye for now."

That evening, after Olivia and Aubrey fell asleep, they each dreamed that they were standing in the town square of Sepadocia. Creedon was sitting there on a throne while the entire city celebrated. And Creedon winked at them.

THE END, FOR NOW

ABOUT THE AUTHOR

Wally Larson, Jr., is an attorney who lives in the Financial District of New York City.

Made in the USA
Monee, IL
26 July 2020

37058172R00114